INCOGNITO
LIFE DOWN UNDER

Other books by
Robert Johnson include:

Choosing Sides
The Epitome of Defeat
The Journey Out of Hell

He also has a downloadable self-help cd titled, *How To Build A Prosperous Life* by Rob Johnson

INCOGNITO
LIFE DOWN UNDER

ROBERT JOHNSON

ARCHWAY
PUBLISHING

Archway Publishing books may be ordered through booksellers or by contacting:

Archway Publishing
1663 Liberty Drive
Bloomington, IN 47403
www.archwaypublishing.com
1 (888) 242-5904

ISBN: 978-1-4808-8630-8 (sc)
ISBN: 978-1-4808-8628-5 (hc)
ISBN: 978-1-4808-8629-2 (e)

Library of Congress Control Number: 2020901122

Print information available on the last page.

Archway Publishing rev. date: 1/25/2020

SUNDAY, 2:00 p.m., and I don't have shit to do. Guess I'll go try to buy me some weed, to calm my nerves and take away the pain while I watch this damn football game. After I buy, I might as well see if somebody around here taking numbers so I can place a bet—fifty on New York, like I do every time the Jets play. Them cats down on David and Jefferson, the Cornell Projects, got the best weed around town. Let me mosey on over there to see what they got. Hope they don't get all scared of a new face and think I'm five-o in shit—you know that's how some niggas think. No, they won't—not if they want this money. They going to serve me. Besides, I'm fitted just enough to look like I just got off work and need something to help me relax. Well, here we go. Let me park my Bentley. Yeah, right. Let me get out of this motherfucking Honda Accord and hope it start back up.

Hey, boss, who got the fire weed?

"Here you go, doc. What you need?"

I just need two dimes or a quo, and I'll be straight.

"You ain't the law, is you, man?"

Hell no. I just got off work at the factory over in Uptown. I'm trying to get me something so I can go home smoke, watch the game, and try to find a nice piece to run up in—that's all.

"Cool, here you go. That'll be twenty-five bones, player."

All right, my name Incognito. Who you be so I know who to ask for next time I come around? Probably tomorrow, the day after.

"Just come. I'll be here."

All right boss, I feel you. Thanks. I'll holler later.

Man, that was easier than I thought. I know this shit ain't going take long. I won't worry about playing my numbers today. The game almost on. I don't want to miss nothing. Shit, I need to clean this place up. It smells like dirty clothes in here. I'll do it after the game. Let me roll this up so I can get into my zone. Damn, this shit better than a bitch. I feel high as hell sitting here tripping off this game. These punk-ass players fumbling the ball, dropping passes. I hope they ass get benched or something, shit. I can't believe they losing like this, 28 to 3. I'm going to take a nap so I can go to the club to-night. Matt's over on Thirty-Fifth be jumping. Plenty of hoes be in there, and besides, I know Darius going to be there—he at the club from Wednesday through Sunday.

9:18 p.m.? Man, I slept a long time. Let me hop in the shower so I can get out of here. I guess I could wear my burgundy Guess jeans, eggshell-white Guess shirt, and white dookies. Put on some smell-good, brush the waves in, and I'm out.

The line is long, just as I suspected. It's going take at least a half an hour to get in here. Glad it's not too cold. For the middle of fall, it's nice—just a small warm breeze, about fifty-five degrees. The line's moving drastically. I'm about the tenth person now, as opposed to thirty-something. I hope when I get in there I get to dance with Jackie, the fine-ass redbone I met while walking up to the line. She was with four of her girls, all looking fine as hell, but she was hella fine. The kind of fine that makes you want to spend all your money on and be crying cause you broke the next day and didn't even get none. Long silky hair, clear light skin, perfect round breasts, thin waist, ass pleasantly round, and just thick in the thighs ... damn, I'm in love. No, but I do want to hit, maybe even taste if it smell, look, and feel good.

Finally, at the front of the door and it's packed inside. Time to get my mack on.

As I entered the room leading to the bar for my drink, I noticed Jackie standing a far distance away across the room. She was pushing away some nigga trying to spit-game. I played it cool by just watching her. I wanted to see how many cats she was going turn away. She turned away at least five that I remember, so now it was time for me to make my move. I slid in her direction with drink already in hand so I wouldn't have to walk back after I asked her if she wanted one. I bought her a ladies' favorite—sex on the beach—and she was all too happy. We talked through a couple of songs, then the alcohol kicked in. We both was ready to dance.

As she pulled me by my hands to the dance floor, all I could think about was hittin' it from the back, as she was deliciously shaped, figure showing all curves in her tightly-fitted black dress. She wasn't a bad dancer, kinda nasty on the floor—wasn't scared to get up close and show what she was working with. She had me ready for whatever as she was gyrating her butt on my manhood and rubbing the back of my head moving to the beat of DJ Quick. We danced through four songs easily before heading to a table to sit down.

As the conversation started to get good, her girlfriends came back, so she gave me her work number to contact her. I was amazed she was fine *and* had a job. I thought she would have been one of them baby-daddy-drama, Jerry-Springer soap-opera hood rats. Well, I took the number and told her I would call sometime later in the week. I could see her girlfriends' faces as I walked away, and from the look of one of them, they was already trying to throw salt. I already had much to drink, so I left.

I got home and went straight to sleep. The next morning, I was feeling every bit of the Tanqueray I drank last night. My head was throbbing with pain, and my stomach was begging for something to eat—some greasy sausages, eggs, and pancakes topped off with a glass of orange juice. Yeah, I hooked it up. After eating, I thought I better get to work, even though I was already fifteen minutes late—what the hell, they ain't gonna fire nobody as bad as they need motherfuckers to work for they minimum-wage-paying asses. I was a pallatizer for a printing company, meaning I loaded finished print materials on a wooden pallet and wrapped it so it could be shipped. I started out working on the day shift, then was moved to third shift, the graveyard. I had a lot of fun working there, although it wasn't too long. I only worked a total of two months before being let go. Life goes on.

Since I was fired at the beginning of my shift, I went straight home to roll up. I needed to relieve some stress. I hit the joint hard and long—a real smoker's hit. The potency of the weed gave me an instant high. I was in a different stratosphere, watching a fucking soccer game that wasn't even speaking no English. I watched the game until one team won. Didn't know the name, just knew they were wearing green and yellow. I thought I better get some weed for later that night just in case something popped off with a honey or something, so I went back to the spot to buy.

Them niggas in Cornell was deep and had all the good shit. They sure was plugged. Only if I knew who they was plugged by so I could get down too, that shit 'a be hella tight. At the spot my man remembered me, so I didn't get no slack—he even gave me some dap. I bought two quos (quarter ounces). This time, I felt so comfortable I introduced myself. I stayed and talked a little bit, had them laughing about the small town I was from. He must have been comfortable too, cause he gave me a nickname, Hog-Mog. He and about six other dudes out there with him was cracking up and making jokes too. I went along with it—hell, the stuff was funny. I left because they started getting real busy, and I didn't want to be in the way.

I went to the mall to do a little shopping for girls and clothes and to eat. I always ate at the Japanese restaurant when I went to the mall—only food that tastes good. The mall was in the suburbs but was patronized by people mainly from the ghetto. I guess the well-to-do folk said it's too many hoodlums going there, so they shop at the more lucrative mall way out don't no ghetto folks drive to cause they end up getting stopped by the cops.

It was a nice crowd for today being a weekday. Some nice honeys walking by, smelling good. I know I'm going pull one, just waiting for the right one. I see her up by the Gap store, so I walk a little faster to catch up. As she made her way into the store, I followed behind as if I was going to buy something out of the store. As she stopped by the jeans, I went over by the shirts. I picked one up and walked over to her to see if she would tell me how it looked. I asked her if she thought it was a good color for me, a little game just to spark up a conversation.

She replied, "It looks fine, but a burgundy. It would look better if the shirt was red."

I said thank you and introduced myself. As we shook hands, she told me her name was Roxanne. We exchanged telephone numbers and parted.

I thought about her on the way to the car but the thought faded when I thought about Jackie fine ass, who I was going to call tonight for sure. I had seen some crazy shit while I was driving home, two men fighting in the middle of the street, holding up traffic. One of the men had blood running all down his face must have got cut on the top of his eye because he was getting whooped. When I finally got past all that, I thought to myself how it's some fucked-up people in the world who need a lot of help, Jesus, or some medication. Damn! I parked the car and ran in the house because it was kind of chilly out today. Wasn't but fifty degrees outside, and I didn't have on a jacket. I threw my bags down, pressed play on the answering machine, and went to piss out some of that large lemonade I had.

While the messages were playing, I heard one from Roxanne, the chick from the mall. Shorty must have been really digging me or lonely to call that quick. Maybe she was just seeing if I gave her the right number. Anyway, I wasn't ready to call her. I was thinking about calling Jackie, so I did.

"Hello, can I talk to Jackie?"

"This is her. Who is this?"

"Michael from Matt's the other night."

"Oh, hey, boo. What's up?"

"Nothing, just chillin. Thought about you."

"Thought about me, what you thought?"

"What you were doing tonight and how good you looked in that black dress."

"Is that right? Well, I isn't doing nothing, and thanks."

"Yeah, I know this nice little place over on Jackson Street. They got some good ass food too."

"What time can I pick you up?"

"Around seven."

"Okay, see you then."

She gave me her address before we hung up to my surprise, because I thought she was going say no, but I was happy she didn't.

It was already going on four, so I had to hurry up and jump in the shower so I could hit the barbershop to get a nice cut. I wanted to look extra tight so I could leave a lasting impression on her, maybe even get some tonight.

I didn't know how this new barber was cutting, so I wanted to make sure I got a chance to see some of the work. I got there in fifteen minutes. The dudes were tight. I have to admit, they were good. I seen three heads get cut by a different two of the four barbers and was impressed. I got in the chair of the owner of the shop because he was good with the straight razor, and I like to have a smooth-as-a-baby-bottom shave. The ladies like that, and it looks good when you have a nice lining and good fit. Plus, the smell-good goes on better. After I got cut and shaved, I paid the bill and gave a tip left and rode around looking for some flowers before heading to pick up Jackie.

Jackie lived all the way on the other side of town, so I had to rush on the expressway to get there in time. I didn't want to be late. I made it to her house to be surprised at what I had seen thus far. She had a beautiful two-story brick home with well-kept landscaping. I peeked in at the back yard before I rang the doorbell just to see if it was as big as the fence hiding it was. I rang the doorbell and was answered by intercom to the sound of Jackie's voice. Jackie opened the door with a smile, as if she had just seen a family member or loved one she hadn't seen in a while.

She was looking astonishing, just as I had expected or fantasized, in her sheer gray after-five dress, black high heels, and fruitful fragrance, blended with her natural body odor. As we began walking to the dining room after my invite in, I noticed she was not wearing any panties as the light hit her backside, which was pleasantly appetizing, as it bounced around just enough to make me want to bite it. During my look, I became aroused, and now had to hide it so she wouldn't notice. Didn't want her to know she had me hooked already. She gave me a tour of the premises as we made small talk. We kept each other laughing as we talked about her house, our work, her outfit, and the day's events. I was surprised at how relaxed she was, and even me for that matter, because I am usually shy around beautiful women. She grabbed her coat and told me she made reservations at a restaurant over on Jackson Street, The African Hut. When she told me the name, I laughed. I didn't know they had a special food. I asked her what they serve, fried zebra or lion. She laughed and said, "No, silly, they got some great chicken dishes, pork, fish, and vegetarian." I was cool with it and just laughed all the way to the car.

I opened the door to see if she would unlock the other doors for me, which she did. That was a good thing, because if she didn't, that would mean she was selfish. Glad she not. In the car, I let her pick the radio station she wanted to listen to just to get a better feel for her personality. She picked an oldies station—another test she passed. Showed she had class but knew how to get loose and wild but kept it at the club, because all they play is fast club-type songs. The ride wasn't long because it was close to her house, about two miles.

We pulled up to valet parking and a nice decor on the outside. The inside was nice and cozy. Had dimmed lighting, candles lit on every table, and white tablecloths. I could tell she frequented the place because as the waiter greeted her, he asked if she would like to sit at her usual table. So we sat at the table far in the back, away from most of the patrons but not secluded. We were served some great fried cheese balls as appetizers to dip in a mildly spiced tomato sauce. During eating, we got a little more in depth with our conversation, learning more about each other's goals, dreams, fantasies, and past relationships. After we got finished eating our curry chicken served on top rice pilaf and a glass of red wine, we was ready for the club.

The club of choice tonight was not Matt's but Club Erogenous. Erogenous was in the same downtown location as the Hut. I had never been to Erogenous but heard a lot about it. Jackie was more of a nightlife person, I guess because she had to relieve some of the stress she endured from her corporate accounting job she did in the day. We didn't have to wait in the long line. Apparently, she had VIP with the club bouncer. He even called her by her name. I thought to myself, *This chick is connected.* This was an elegant club too. It had neon lights circling the floor, the ceiling lights just dimmed enough to see one another, the right music playing, just great. We did have to wait some time for our drinks because the servers were very busy filling other orders. Finally, we received our drinks—two sex on the beaches and a bottle of Moët—after twenty minutes passed. The drinks were nice, just what I needed to get me a little more relaxed and social. Alcohol always did that to me.

I was now feeling like God's gift to women. I knew I was going be sleeping on her sheets tonight. We danced awhile, finished off the bottle of Champagne, and left. During the drive home, the conversation got heated. We started talking about what positions we liked the best, which ones we tried, and what gets each other aroused. I was really aroused when she told me she liked it missionary and doggy style, just the way I like to give it. As we were approaching her house, she took my hand and placed it between her thighs right on her wet spot. As she glided my hand up and down her wet vulva, she looked me up and down with a devilish smile.

2

M Y place is a wreck. I have to clean up before the landlord comes to collect the rent. Don't want her—or anybody, for that matter—to think I am a pig. I have clothes lying everywhere, old pizza box on the counter, beer bottles on the coffee table—takes me back to my sorority days, before I matured. Man, this is a mess. This is not like me, but it is kind of cool to be outside of my meticulous neat-freak mode. Toss this in here for the laundry, garbage bag all of this in the refrigerator and vacuum across the floor, a touch of air freshener, and everything is back to normal. All of thirty minutes, just in time for Mrs. Holland's 12:30 visit, which she keeps every fifteenth day of the month because I'm always late with the rent.

Mrs. Holland is a fine-ass lady, nicely built to be in her forties. She never says forty what, just, "Forty-something, young man." I bet her husband still likes to hit that because I wouldn't mind she come by here smelling good and dressed nice every visit. Speaking of here, she is coming to the door now.

"Hey, Mrs. Holland."

"Hey, boy, where the rent with your late-paying ass?"

"I got the check right here, dang."

"Good. You know I love you, right? I got to give you some hassle. You always late."

"Yeah I know, I'm sorry too, but my funds don't clear until the fifteenth. Plus, I like to see you."

"Uh-hum, I bet. See you next month—unless something goes wrong."

"All right."

I'm glad she not one of those snooping all-in-your-business slum landlords. She just come get the rent, make sure ain't no complaints, especially drug or repairs needed, and be on her merry way. Must be nice to have money to live like that worry-free. I'll be like that one of these broke-ass days. Speaking of broke, I better get dressed so my broke ass can go looking for a job, which I should've been doing early this morning.

I still have time to get over to a couple of places. I'll start at the mall with some department stores. They always in need of some fine salespeople. Ain't no way they going turn me away with this nice knock-off Brooks Brothers suit. I might even be able to get an interview and job acceptance today if I run into the right manager. Hope so.

Driving down this strip to get to the mall is faster. I never knew about this route. I took Spencer all the way up to Edgewood, where the mall is located. Usually I hopped on the expressway only to go around the loop, which took me a mile out of the way. It's a shame how a lot of people just hanging out not doing nothing. I wonder how they surviving. I guess they all got some hustle going on or something, but hell, I ain't going to even try to figure it out, cause it would take forever or drive me crazy trying. The mall was empty—usually is during the week. I'll be in and out of here quick. I got three stores on my agenda that I want to apply at first, cause the last time I was here, the manager at one of them told me they was in need of a manager. Shoreline, Tight Bottom, and Exquisite Looks were the stores that needed a manager—all stores that sold to predominately black customers. I'm sure one of them is going to hire me.

I went to Exquisite Looks first because that is the store I really want to work at. Glad I did, cause the manager was on duty, so I could get my interview right away, just like I hoped. The interview took ten minutes, and I walked out of there with a job. I didn't need to go to the other stores, because this was full-time, forty hours a week—thank *God*.

Now I need to celebrate hit up the weed spot: Cornell Projects. The same people out here all the time. They need a real job. Hog-Mog in the house let me get a quo.

"Here you go, country-ass nigga," one of the dudes said as we exchanged money for product. It was fluffy and green, as usual.

"I been coming round long enough. What's y'all names, man. At least I can get that. I might want to take y'all out for a drink or something. You know, go kicking it."

As they passed an already lit blunt to me, the names came out. The one who passed it to me first said, "I'm Scooby."

To his left, "I'm Do-Dirt."

"Red."

And finally the leader of the crew spoke his name: "Silencer."

I hit the blunt a few times and passed it. Silencer asked, "Where you live, Hog?"

"On Twenty-Third and Wells, just a little apartment for now."

*   *   *

I don't know where I'm going. I'm just driving. That was my first time smoking outside like that in the middle of the day. I feel kind of strange. I hope this fade off soon. I'm too high. I guess I'll go get my cell phone I been telling myself I was going get for the last month. I think I'm going to get this camera one I seen on the Sprint commercial. It was small and could take pictures while folded by the press of a button. It cost $100, which was reasonable compared to the other phones. I chose this little blue one. I called Jackie to give her my number so she could reach me if she wanted in case I wasn't at the crib. She was at work, so we didn't talk long, but she agreed to hook up later. Told me to meet her at her house at six. I wasn't hesitant in complying to her demand, because I immediately thought about the night we shared together last night. She was more than a freak in bed—she was an animal. She rode me, sucked me, rode me some more, took it missionary, doggy, and even froggy style before gushing out a massive tidal wave of sweet vagina juice over my penis. Her orgasm lasted for three whole minutes.

I don't know why she was single, but I was glad. Hopefully she wouldn't be for too much longer. I drove back to my place to chill until it was time for Jackie to get off work so I could meet her. I ended up dozing off on the couch once back at the apartment, watching the National Geographic channel, which I liked to watch frequently because of the shows aired required you to think and expand your horizons a little. I get tired of watching the same old junk on the local network channels. They be about the same stuff all the time: sex, money, music. Although they be good shows, just need something different now and again. I remember having a dream about mating and animal rituals. The animals in my dream were some of the people I know. The pack that Jackie and I belonged to was a pack of rhinoceroses. I was the head, and she was the lead. We were separated by divisions in the shallow waters surrounding us. It began to get good when we started mating in the water. I mounted her from behind and gave her all I had, getting a loud, thunderous moan with every thrust. That's when I woke up, because I thought I had ejaculated on myself. How embarrassing that would have been—a twenty-five-year-old man having a wet dream.

Well, it's good I woke, because it's now time to go get the real stuff. Time to meet Queen Jackie. I was waiting for her to pull up so I could greet her with the single red rose I had to show my emotions for her. She pulled shortly after I got there with a card in hand for me. Looks like we were thinking about each other. Must have been good to her too. We greeted each other with a hug and a kiss. We went into her house so she could get into some after-work clothes. I watched her undress in amazement. I immediately remembered my dream and wanted to mount her voluptuous bottom as she bent over to slide off her pantyhose. So I did what the rhinoceros did and mounted. She gave a slight moan as I gently entered her already moist cave. With one hand caressing her left breast and the other hand clutching her hair, I began to go in and out faster. I was now painlessly pounding the womanly G-spot, and she was now talking in tongues as if she was demon-possessed as she began talking dirty to me, cursing and telling me to fuck her harder. I did as told, and with one hand still on her breast, we both climaxed.

After the shower we took to rid each other of the scent of sex, we got in her car for a drive. I didn't ask where we were going, because I trusted in her to take me wherever she wanted. We talked and laughed while listening to the radio. The drive was getting long, and then we pulled up in front of this beautiful big two-story—what looked like a mansion. It was neatly landscaped with a huge yard. The other houses on the block were just as gorgeous. When she told me, "Let's go," I asked who we were going to see. She said, "I want you to meet my mother."

I really wasn't ready for that but didn't want to disappoint her, so I followed her lead. She must have knew I was nervous, because she told me to relax—her mother ain't no mean person. She had the key, so we went straight in. She yelled out, "Janice, yo daughter here, and I got a friend, so put on some clothes."

I laughed and said, "Y'all must be real close for you to call her that."

She replied, "Yeah, we got a good relationship. My mom real cool. Think she still young."

"How old is she?"

"Fifty-two."

"She is young."

"Yeah, right."

"No, that's kind of old, but she still active and fun like she young."

As she came walking down the stairs, I thought to myself that she still look good, like she young. If I didn't know, I would not have thought she was fifty-two. I could see where Jackie got her looks and body. They almost look like twins. Jackie introduced us.

"Momma, this is my friend Michael. Michael this is my mother, Janice."

"Hi, Janice."

"Hi, Michael. So you dating my daughter, huh."

"I don't know. She didn't tell me yet."

"Hell, you are you here ain't you. And you screwing her, right. So, you dating her."

Jackie interjected, "Momma, leave him alone. Michael, don't pay her no mind. She just being nosy."

I laughed as they began talking, and her mother hugged me, saying, "Young man, just treat her good. She a good woman. I know because I raised her."

They chatted I listened and occasionally spoke, mostly laughed at they conversation cause it was so friendly and untraditional—at least, for me it was.

As we were leaving, I saluted her with a "It was nice meeting you," while Jackie stated, "I'll call you."

When we got in the car, Jackie asked me, "Well, what did you think of my mother?"

I said, "I thought she was great, but y'all got a funny-in-a-good-way relationship.

She replied, "Yeah, everybody say that, but that's my momma. We just cool like that ever since I was a little girl."

"That's good. A lot people don't even talk to they mother or father, let alone joke with them. That's tight y'all like that. So, you think she like me?"

"Hell, yeah. That's why I took you over there."

"How you know she like me?"

"Because she was nonchalant with you. She joked about you fucking me. If she didn't like you, she would have just said hi."

"Oh. Well, I'm glad she like me. So, do you like me?"

"You ahight."

"Ahight?"

"Yeah, I like you, silly. If I didn't, you wouldn't have got none. I liked you the moment I saw you."

"Cool, so do that mean we dating?"

"Do you want to?"

"Yeah."

"Well, you my nigga. We dating. You bet not let me catch you talking to another chick, cause my ugly going to come out, and you don't want that. Okay?"

"Okay. Ah, shit. Don't tell me you got different personalities."

"I got about three people in my head, but they only come out when necessary."

"You crazy."

"Just a little bit."

"I'm just playing. But for real, don't cheat on me and I'll be the best thing that ever happened to you."

When she said that, it kind of did something to me. I had never had a woman tell me something like that before. I fell for her right there, at that moment. She opened my heart up a little. We stopped at the video store to get a couple of movies to watch for the rest of the now rainy night. We got a comedy, a romance, and an action, along with some popcorn and candy. She had the drink already, some good old fashioned Kool-Aid. That's one of the things I liked about Jackie. She had a nice paying job but still drank Kool-Aid. We finished all three movies, cuddled up on the lounge sofa she had. It was comfortable enough to be a bed. After the movies, we took a shower together and went to bed.

The next morning, I woke before her to surprise her with breakfast in bed. I made pancakes and a cheese omelet. She didn't have any sausage or bacon. I put enough for her and me on a plate with a glass of orange juice and walked it to her. I woke her out of half-sleep by calling her name.

"I made us breakfast."

She replied, "You didn't have to do that."

"I know, but I wanted to. Taste it. It's going make you melt. I'm a great cook."

She tasted the omelet and said, "You can cook this better than the restaurant."

"Thank you, baby."

She was already running late thanks to our morning round of good-day sex. Sex was always good in the morning to me. I think that's when women are more moist and aroused. I was half-asleep not paying any attention to the time or the fact that Jackie had already left the house. When I rolled over and looked at the clock, it was 8:30. I jumped out of bed and got in my clothes, realizing I was late for work.

I still had to stop at the apartment because I didn't have a change of clothes at Jackie's place, so now I was going to be even more late than I was already. I got in the apartment and ran straight in the bedroom to grab something out of the closet to put on. No time for a shower—just throw on some deodorant and couple spritzes of cologne. Nobody going know but me anyway. I ran back to the car. I was now an hour late. I couldn't call the store because I was supposed to open. No one was scheduled until 12:00. What kind of manager is late opening the store?

I was hoping nobody was waiting at the door to get in because I would be shit with the boss if he got word of it. He was some bigshot from an upscale neighborhood. Didn't care about nothing but money and more money. I pulled in the parking lot at 11:37. The store was supposed to be open at ten o'clock with the other stores in the mall. I know I'm a hear some shit about this, but what can I say. Just hope I don't get fired. Wasn't nobody waiting, which was a good thing, but the owner called three times. I forgot I was supposed to fax over the reports from the previous day before opening so his accountant can do the books. Shit, I know I am so fired.

I made it through the entire day. I laughed with Tommy, the salesperson, about being late and why. He called me crazy for not getting up out of the pussy when I was supposed to. Even told me, "Hope she got a good job, cause your ass going to get fired. Happened to another manager before being late and all. Said he was late coming from his doctor appointment. The boss didn't care."

Sure enough, he called me before closing and told me the job needed someone that was going to be there on time, because there was money to be made from opening to closing. He told me leave my key with the other manager that was coming shortly. Oh well, I got one week worth of pay coming.

The manager came, collected the belongings, and closed up. I didn't even worry about the reports. Let him do it. I called Jackie when I left to tell her what happened. She laughed at me, saying, "My shit that good you can't get out of bed," before telling me don't worry about it—she going to see who in her network of people know somebody hiring. It was amazing how supportive and down-to-earth this chick was. I had never experienced it in all my days of dating. I mean, she wasn't afraid to admit her faults, her likes, and even her freaky side without knowing somebody for years. Maybe it was just me she was comfortable with, or maybe she just looking for a man. I don't think she looking for a man, cause she hella fine and got a job, so she a magnet for men. I don't know what it is, but I'll take it.

Before I went to her house, I stopped to kick it with Silencer and the crew. They were up to the same old shit—hanging out, dealing, smoking, and fucking with the hoes that everybody had already fucked. Hell they had all probably fucked the same hoes, probably all at the same time too, which explains why Do-Dirt always scratching. I kicked it for a long time this time, just getting to know them a little better and letting them know me—at least, what I wanted them to know. I even hollered at some hoes, not that I was really interested, just to see if I could get them. I have to admit, it was some fine thick ones out just hanging.

I seen some thug girls before, but these took the cake. It was cool, though, because I like them jazzy with a little attitude but still ladylike—just turns me on. During the length of our conversation, I began asking my new compadres how they got they nicknames, only to get some not-so-shocking responses. Do-Dirt got his name cause that's what he always did: dirt. Whether he was screwing somebody wife or girlfriend, he was jacking somebody. Scooby got his name just because he had big ears and everybody said he sound like Scooby-Doo. Red, simply because he was red. You know real light, with reddish-brown hair. The infamous one-and-only Silencer—just what it sounds like. He shut motherfuckers up for good.

The thing that was shocking about Silencer was he was not a

big dude at all. Matter of fact, he was kind of skimpy but stout. He was quiet and laid back, with some fierce eyes. When you look him in the eyes, it was like looking at a ghost with fiery pupils, so most became nervous and didn't talk much. I guess that's why he was Silencer. I also picked up some game watching them take care of business serving the customers that came up.

Depending on what was needed, one would take the money during a handshake, and somebody else would give the drugs, or "product," in another handshake. Just to throw the cops and whoever else was watching. The customers would shake everybody hand to make it look like they was showing some love, saying "What's up?" It was a smooth operation. After I smoked to the max, over-clouding my brain, I decided to leave. I gave some dap to everybody and parted to the heckling of them all: "Later. You gotta learn to hang with the big boys. We only smoked one blunt."

"Yeah, but that blunt was filled to the max. Later."

I got to Jackie's house with the munchies, desperately in need of some grub. I raided the cabinets and refrigerator for some chips, sandwich meat, and something to drink. I made myself a big bologna-turkey-cheese hoagie, with a side of chips and glass of apple juice. I was eating not only to fill my craving but to take the high away before Jackie came home. Don't know how she would handle me being high in her house or around her. I was laid out on the bed, knocked out after taking a shower. I woke up to the surprise of a warm mouth around my penis. She just always seems to find a way to amaze me every time we together. I was now wide awake and erect, ready to explode. As I began to pull away, doing the gentleman thing, she grabbed my erection tightly and placed her full lips around the head until every last drop of cum was done secreting. I was in love and in heaven all at the same time. Since Jackie came in surprised me with the ultimate hook-up, it was only right I reciprocated. I eased off her clothes, beginning with her shirt and bra so I could get to her breasts. I began sucking her nipples, both in my mouth at the same time.

After realizing she was highly aroused, I slid off her skirt and panties, beginning to kiss my way down to her feet. I stayed at her navel, then went down one leg at a time, sucking her toes. I came back up the inside, gently biting her inner thighs. Now I was at the love box. It smelled oh so good, I couldn't help kissing it, then sucking in the already heavy flowing juices. She tasted so sweet, I stuck my tongue inside, twirling it around like I was licking a plate of my favorite dish. She was now ecstatic and shaking as I blew her clitoris and sucked it as she juiced a heavy orgasm.

I thought she would be done, but as she felt my still hard penis, she got on all fours and told me to hit that shit, to which I gladly obliged. We went at it, switching positions for an hour or so until we both climaxed. Now exhausted, we just lay there, holding each other. She asked the question, "So, who you smoke some weed with?"

I was stuck. I didn't think she knew. At least, I know she ain't dumb. I told her just some fellas around the way. I thought she was going to get into why I shouldn't do it and don't bring it to her house, but instead, she asked if I had any for her. I laughed, saying, "What, you smoke?"

She replied, "Yeah, on occasion. I don't have to worry about getting dropped at work, so why not. Besides, it help me relax when I had a hard, long day. But I don't do it often."

I rolled up a joint to smoke with her as we continued talking. It just felt good laying next to her smooth, curvy body.

I had not done that in such a long time with someone I felt connected to. While we were smoking, she suggested I move in with her. I asked if she was serious. She told me that is what she gave me the key for. I agreed. She told me I could do anything I wanted there. Just don't have no other woman, especially in her house, or don't have backstabbing jealous niggas in there either. I agreed.

She began opening up to me telling me her whole life, from childhood to adulthood. She told about how she would have to play by herself as a child because her mother was always working and her grandmother, who would be babysitting, didn't allow her friends to come in the house. Then she started telling me how she would make up imaginary friends to play with. I asked if she talked to them and laughed when she told me yes. I didn't mean to, but it was funny and sad. I told her I felt her pain, and listened further as she told me about her school life. When she was a teenager, the girls at school would pick on her and always want to fight because she was prettier, more developed, and smarter than them. She told me about how all the boys would be after her too—another reason they didn't like her. I was sentimental in telling her she been through a lot. I asked her questions like how she dealt with all of that. Didn't she have cousins or sisters to play with? And did she have any dolls or toys? She told me she played with her cousins at barbecues, but that was it, and then not all time because they weren't close either. I felt sorry for her. It seemed like she had a horrible life. I was relieved when she began telling me about her brother, whom she was close with but didn't see much, and her high school friends, whom she was still acquainted with to this day.

She went back to the night we were at the club, telling me two of the girls with her had been her best friends since high school. They even went to the same college together. That it is some cool shit. You don't find many men that went to the same high school and college together still friends long after they graduated.

I asked her a little about her brother before telling her about me. She told me very little, just told me he was always a loner as a kid, except for a few neighborhood friends he had. She didn't see him much, mainly during the holidays.

I began telling her my life story, which wasn't anywhere near as harsh as hers. I told her I grew up with just my mother and father in a small two-bedroom house that my mother sold after my father passed away when I was in the twelfth grade. I told her we were very close, always played board games together and watched TV shows or rented movies. I told her I had friends, but a lot of them ended up moving off to other states after college to pursue their careers. My mother died two years after I moved here. When I asked her about her father, she told me she didn't know much about him. He left when she was seven years old and never came back. That ended our talking for the night. We went to sleep naked, joined in arms like conjoined twins.

I knew that I had to treat her right. I liked the way she made me feel. The feeling I got from her was something like no other. I mean, when I even thought of her, I got a tingly chill through my body.

The next morning, Jackie awoke before me, preparing me breakfast this time. I awoke to the smell and followed my nose to the kitchen, where my plate was already made and waiting for me on the table. I didn't have to be told to sit down. I just did and devoured the deliciously prepared breakfast.

Talking over breakfast, Jackie planned out the day for us. We were to go to the art museum to view a new art exhibit (Jackie had a liking for good art), to the mall for some shopping, and to a movie and dinner. I had nothing to do but go along with her plans. She was the boss, and I could not have come up with a better one.

The museum was nice. I had never been to the museum before, so seeing the art exhibits opened my mind up to the different cultures around the world. We looked at the main one we had come to see—some rare carvings from a tiny tribal village in coastal Africa. Then we looked at some paintings, some statues and finally an exhibit from Egypt containing King Tut, Cleopatra, the Sphynx, and other Egyptian sculptures. We ended our visit on a good note and headed to the mall.

We didn't go to the mall uptown but opted to go on the highway to one located in a suburb on the outskirts of the county line. The mall was huge, with all the major department stores. We window-shopped and bought some items before taking a break to sit down in the food court. We indulged ourselves in the fine food of pretzels and lemonade. I got a raisin pretzel, and she a cinnamon. Even watching her shop was fun. She wasn't like the typical "take-forever woman." She looked at something and knew if she wanted it right away. I was pleased to be a help to her by giving my opinion when asked. She told me the best way to shop was to have someone of the opposite sex or a gay person with you, because they liked to see someone attractive in the outfit. I laughed at that statement, saying, "Well, I don't think I'll have a gay dude with me, but I see your point."

She just laughed and pinched me on the butt.

We left the mall with our bags headed for the movies. We didn't plan what we were going to see, just went on impulse. We ended up watching some comedy stand up. It was funny as all get-out. Jackie was crying she laughed so hard. It was as if she had not had a good laugh in a long time. I didn't bother to ask about it. I was just happy to see someone so happy. I laughed at it too, but I didn't really appreciate it much because my mind was not fully there. I was pre-occupied with other thoughts. My first thought was of my wife and kids, which Jackie didn't know I had. I had forgotten about them too because I had to. Then I was thinking about Silencer and the crew. And of course, how soon it would be before I got to Darius Brown, the big-time drug pusher I was obligated to take down.

You see, Jackie didn't know I was already working for the FBI. Nor did anyone else, because I had only enough clout to contact the department every so often. I didn't contact Marcy and the kids because I had to tell myself they were dead to deal with the fact that I could not see them or be with them to keep them protected and to stay focused. Working undercover was always dangerous because if you blew your cover it could cost you your life and anyone close to you—usually your family if you were onto someone big. I thought I had had all the memories out, but sitting next to Jackie in the the-atre made me think of Marcy, because we frequented the movies, so I had to snap out of it and get back into the role. I grabbed Jackie by the hand to draw her in close to me so I could give her a kiss. As she got close enough, I put my hand around her kissing her and told her I loved her. The look in her eyes was that of someone who had just been proposed to. She told me she loved me too and con-tinued to watch the movie. The movie ended shortly after, which was good, because I was hungry. We didn't go anywhere fancy for dinner; just some good old-fashioned hole-in-the-wall helped me to get back into undercover mode. I told her to let me pick the place for dinner since she had picked the museum, movie, and shopping.

I picked a joint called Harry's, a nice little chicken and fish shack on the border of the hood and the suburbs. Harry's made famous for the great greasy fresh fish and chicken, served with your choice of wafer fries or shoestring fries and sweet potato pie. Harold, the owner, was a Jewish dude in his fifties but still got around like he was twenty. Jackie had never been here in her adult years but said she remembered coming when she was a teenager with her mother. I was a favorite here. They knew me by name. I ordered my usual— two Cajun-fried thighs and two wings with wafer fries, a slice of butter sweet potato pie, and a glass of squeezed lemonade. Jackie ordered the fish and chips. Dinner went by great. We ate, talked, got full, and went back to Jackie's house.

While Jackie was in the shower, getting ready to display her new negligee, I put on some nice soft jazz, lit some candles, and dimmed the lights. She came out beautiful. The red matching two-piece with garter strap set was stunning on her. I went to take a shower so I could slip into something more comfortable too. I wanted to surprise her with something other than the usual sex we would have. I had bought a bottle of wine at the mall, which I had in the fridge chilling so we could sip and dance once I got out. I took a shower for about five minutes, put on my silk pajama bottoms she had bought for me, and surprised her with the glass of wine. She was ecstatic from the expression on her face. We danced awhile, finished off the bottle of wine, and talked until the wee hours of the morning.

3

BEING back in Belleview makes me think of everything I left behind. I look at the houses, parks, buildings, and everything else that's so common here but missing in Milwaukee. I was called home to brief my commanding officers on what advancements were being made with the Darius case. I was going to be in town for only one day, so I had a lot to accomplish.

I had to meet Marcy and the kids at the arranged meeting place. I couldn't do it at our house, for their protection, in case someone was onto me and followed me. I also had to take care of some meetings with investment partners I had. And last but not least, I had to go to the office, a secluded diner in the hillsides. The command post was set up there because it was unidentifiable to the untrained eye. No one but those in law enforcement would know about it.

The flight in took six hours, including the layover in Phoenix. I got in a nap on the plane, so I was energized ready to take care of business. Marcy and the kids met me in the shopping mall. We had to talk across the room from our cell phones. Whenever I was on assignment and came back into town, we would meet at different sites. This time it was the mall. She played it off as if she were waiting for her husband to come before deciding which movie to see all while talking to me. The conversation was the usual: how have things been going with the kids in school, how are the bills, how much we miss each other, and her telling me to be safe. Then we would head to the theatre to watch a movie of the kids' choosing. We never let them see me because they were too young to understand my job, and it would be too hard to get away from them. After the movie, I went to the investors I was set up with to close on a land development deal. Then I was off to the commander briefing.

I gave the commanding officers my info on the case against Darius, explaining to them I couldn't tie him to anything yet because he was out of sight. He doesn't touch anything or come to the distribution location. All I got was a tap into his main worker, Silencer, and his crew, which was a good start. They gave me new info on what deals were going down and which dealers were making them. I have to admit, they knew a lot, even had pictures of me smoking with the crew. I was impressed. However, they had nothing on Darius either. Nothing even on the upper-level dealers, just street-level and house dealers. After the briefing, I was out, back to the airport, and on the plane.

From the airport, I drove to Cornell to check in on Silencer and the crew. They were inside an apartment that was to be used when it was cold outside. It was getting closer to winter, which meant the thermometer had started to drop. It was around forty or even thirty degrees outside, but with the wind, it felt a lot colder. Other than the lookout boys and a few foot soldiers, it was a ghost town. I had to think of a way to get more acquainted with Silencer so I could work my way into the clique. By doing so, I would definitely work my way to his supplier. So far, I didn't have anything going other than letting him make fun of me to cater to his ego, but in time, I would devise a plan.

I finally got into the apartment after going through security checks. The room was dim from the cloud of weed smoke and blue light. It was a perfect setting if you were a true weed smoker. The sound of Tupac was playing just enough for you to feel the bass and soak in the evocative lyrics. The blue light was bright enough to see everyone and everything without a blur. And as I walked in, the conversation was a mere debate over which of the albums Tupac put out was the best. I joined in the conversation after purchasing my usual quarter ounce of Flyright, the street name for the highly potent strain of weed. The blunts was already there, so I was invited to roll one up, which was a good sign that things were looking up for building trust with the clique. I rolled up one and lit it. I took three pulls off the nicely-rolled stick before passing it to Do-Dirt. When asked which album I liked best, I said without a doubt it was *Strictly 4 My N.I.G.G.A.Z.* I shared the same favorite as Red. He asked me which song was the best on there. I was glad to say "Violent." The song was well versed over the sound of nice drums and cymbals. When listening to it, you instantly got sucked in to what Pac was saying. I asked if they had it in there so we could hear it to keep the debate going and prove Red and my point. Scooby put it on so we could listen to it. When it came on, we all got silent. The room became quiet except for the tunes playing, and if the sound of head nodding could be recorded, you would have heard it. The song played in its entirety without any interruption. After the song ended, in unison, everyone agreed about the tightness of the lyrics and beat. Each of us gave our opinion on which verse was the best. The topic was discussed briefly before another blunt was rolled and the song played again.

This time there was an interruption from a knock on the door. It was some ladies from down the hall, nice-looking young ladies, no more than twenty. It was five of them, three which I remember seeing outside one or more times I visited. The ladies came prepared to kick it. They had some weed and some drink, a bottle of Hennesey and apple juice. It appeared they had already knew who they would be kicking it with, even the fifth lady, because she aggressively came onto me. I was stunned at how she was bold enough to blurt out, "I want to fuck you" after first complimenting me on how good I looked. I was put in a no-punk-out situation, kind of like the time when a buddy of mine took me to a birthday party and told the birthday girl I was the stripper he had arranged for her. I was thinking about Marcy and Jackie, thinking to myself that I was sinking more and more, but I had to in order for the operation to be successful. With Shelly sitting on my lap, I soon forgot about Jackie and Marcy and transfixed on her nice frame and what she was whispering in my ear. After a few nibbles, I was all hers, at least for the time being.

We smoked some more, drank the drink, and before long, the crowd had shrunk. Silencer and his companion had vanished into one of the two bedrooms, and Do-Dirt and his girl the other. Off into a corner of the living room was Scooby and the nicely-built girl he had, leaving Red and me along with our phillies sharing the couch. Red and his girl moved to the chair, already half-naked, to take care of their functions, leaving Shelly and me the whole sofa. While engaged in some heavy kissing, I placed my hand in her panties, becoming immediately hard after feeling her wet, hairy vagina. I fingered her, getting her into the mood a little more to make her ready for my nine inches. Her panties came off, along with her bra, displaying her cone-shaped breasts, bushy vagina, and nicely shaped ass. I lay back as she unzipped my pants, pulling out my manhood, gently stroking it with her soft hands. She went down, placing it in her mouth to my amazement, making me want her more. Fingering herself while sucking, I guess she was now ready to be taken, because she got on top of me and rode me like she was possessed. I came in less than five minutes. That was a first, I guess. It was the thrill of the surprise element of being with a complete stranger and in a room with other people. I can't leave out the fact the vagina was good. I'm glad that didn't happen with Jackie, cause then I would have been embarrassed, probably would not have been able to talk to her again, but with this broad, I cared but I didn't. She was just a fuck that shouldn't have even happened. I blame it on the alcohol. I kind of feel sorry for her, because she seem like a nice girl, just looking for love in all the wrong places. That don't make it no better. I just contributed to her hurt, because I know what just happened ain't going to go nowhere. Maybe I'm thinking too much into the whole situation. She could be wanting just a fuck. Oh well, forget about it. I gotta get going. I told her I would see her next time I came through and thanked her for the sex.

Before leaving, I asked her for her phone number to be nice, but you never know, I just might use it. I told Red I was leaving because I had to get up in the morning and it was getting too late. He hollered, "Later," and continued what he was doing. I called Jackie when I got to the car told her I was on my way over there so she could get ready for me, but she didn't answer the phone. During the drive, I was thinking how I was going to pull this off, going over there this late. It was one in the morning. I just had sex with another woman after she told me not to cheat on her. *Man, I'm stupid. How could I let this happen?*

As I got closer to the house, I began to sweat from the nervousness. What if she waiting up for me? What if she smell the sex on me by smelling my penis, like some women do. As I pulled in front of the house, I was relieved to see her car not there. I hurried up ran into the house to take a shower. I jumped out of my clothes, throwing them down the clothes shute so they could be washed. I turned the shower on hot and rubbed my sex-smelling area with mouthwash to rid it of the smell before I got in the shower. It was funny, I remembered that method. I had heard it from one of my old buddies when he used to cheat on his wife.

While in the shower, I began thinking about all the shit I was doing just to catch somebody who would probably go to jail for a short period, get out, and do the same thing, probably better than he did before after sharing information with other prisoners. I hope it's all worth it and he doesn't get off scot-free. I collected my thoughts and continued washing. I kind of got startled when Jackie stepped in the shower with me. I didn't hear her come in, but I was relieved that the sex smell was gone. She put her arms around me, rubbing my chest, then slid her hands down to my genitals. I asked her in a joking manner where she was at coming in this late by herself.

She replied, "I don't remember you being my daddy or my husband."

I answered her, "I might not be your daddy, but I just might be your husband."

She replied, "You crazy silly boy. I was at Matt's with my friend Vanessa. Where you been?"

"I was with some of the fellas I used to work with at the factory. We went to the strip club."

"The strip club, that means you all ready to handle this, huh?"

"I guess so."

She assumed the position in front of me, hands to ankles so I could enter her womaness. She was enticing me to be hers. Every time, she was always gushing wet, ready for me to fuck her. I didn't mind, because I liked doing it. This was a quickie—lasted all of ten minutes, just enough time for us to both cum. She stood up and kissed me, saying, "Thank you, Daddy." We went to bed without discussing my adventure. I was safe and happy to know she trust me and I could trust her.

I went to sleep thinking about how it would be when it came time to end all of this and go back home to Marcy and the kids. I had never been in a situation such as this. For the most part, when I worked undercover, I never had to stay under. I'd make some quick buys from dealers that our informants told us about, but now, I had a mission that had to be completed, and I just kept slipping further and further into the game. I got myself into a clique, I got a woman who was attached to me (and me to her), and I already had a woman on the side who might be hooked up but whom I had no interest in. I fucked up, but I'll pull it together. I'm the best there is. I'm Incognito.

I woke up a refreshed person. I had the drive I needed to get the ball rolling. I asked Jackie about the job lead she had mentioned. She told me she was working on it, that she knew this guy who was looking for some help at one of his video shops. I was cool to know that. She asked me if I was going to bring the rest of my things over to make it official, since that was what she gave me the key for. Now feeling under pressure, I said yes, I was going to get the remaining things today and turn in the keys. I wasn't looking forward to this, because I now would have to hear Mrs. Holland's bickering about not giving her a month's notice, as required according to my lease, which I would also be breaking. Now I was going to have to do some smooth talking to get my security deposit back and not have her take me to small claims court for breach of contract. I didn't know how I was going to fix this right now, but I'd think of something before she came over. Maybe I'll tell her I have to go on an emergency leave out of town for the rest of the year and can't afford to pay the rent cause I won't be working. She won't believe that shit, and if she does, she probably won't care unless somebody died, and I didn't want to tell that lie. I'll think about what to tell her when she gets over. First, I got to call her.

"Mrs. Holland I need you to come over. I have to talk about my lease."

"What's going on? I'm busy now. I'll be over when I'm finished here in about a hour or two."

"Okay, I'll talk to you when you get here."

I packed while waiting for her, and just as she said, an hour and fifty minutes later, she was there. I opened the door, kind of nervous cause I hadn't come up with nothing to tell her as the reason of me moving, and I didn't have no money to pay for my lease, being broke. She seen all the garbage bags everywhere, and things unplugged.

"You know, since you moving, you breaking your lease by three months, don't you?" I said I know but I got to move. She said, "You going pay for the three months."

"I really don't have the money. That's why I gotta move. I'm moving in with a friend till I get another job."

"Yeah right. Your ass met some heffa you moving in with. Who you think you fooling, as fine as your ass is. I know how the game go. I ain't that old, boy."

"So that mean you going let me slide?"

"It ain't that easy. I'm going to let you off by not taking you to court, but you have to work for it."

"That's fine. When do you want me to start?"

She smiled, taking off her coat and said, "Now."

I laughed. "What you want me to do?"

"It's been a long time since I had my vagina ate real good. I want you to eat my vagina till I cum, and then I want to pee on you."

"Damn, Mrs. Holland, you a freak."

"I told you, I ain't that old. Can you handle that?"

"I guess so … if I'm going to get out of my lease. But what Mr. Holland going say?"

"Who said he going to know?"

"Okay, let's do this."

I ate her vagina like I never ate vagina before, and she sure wasn't lying when she hadn't had it ate in a long time, because she was squeezing my head with her thighs and squirming all over the place, moaning and groaning until she squirted out a thick white creamy nut. After she was finished, she had me to lay there for her to pee on me. I have to admit, I had never had to do that, before but it turned me on. I would have to ask Jackie if I could do it with her. Mrs. Holland thanked me for my services before leaving, telling me to leave the keys on the table when I left.

Standing, there still bedazzled by what had just gone down, I looked at her and said, "Sure thing." I enjoyed every moment of the sexcapade, even without me penetrating her or cumming myself. I did wonder how a beautiful woman, full of youth, such as herself, couldn't get satisfied at home. Maybe he was doing his stuff on the side, or maybe he couldn't get it up no more. I don't know and didn't care—not for me to worry about. I took my belongings out to the car, heaviest stuff first so I could get it out of the way, making it easier to get the lighter bags. Looking at the now-empty apartment, I didn't know if I was making the right decision moving in with Jackie. She was nice looking, good in bed, even supportive and helpful, but that's how they all start out. What if she is really a bitch that don't clean up until company coming over? Or what if she nags and complains about every little thing? Maybe she farts in bed or belches out loud while watching TV. No, I'm tripping. I would have seen those signs already. It's going be hard to keep in contact with Marcy now. Shit. But it's my job. I got to do it, although I don't think the company approves of this type shit. But fuck it, I want this case over.

I have a lot of work to do, but I'm not pressured because things are going smoothly. I got inside the inner circle of a clique that is moving things. I made a name for myself here. Surely it won't be long before I get connected to Darius. I'll get my cake and eat it too. Moving in with Jackie will give the opportunity to move up faster too because I can save the money I was using for the apartment rent to put toward buy money. The money the department gave undercovers was very limited. We had to hustle the rest, just like other dealers. I never worked this side of narcotics before—usually prescription drugs or making a buy from corner dealers—but it's all the same: you against them. I was glad to do what I do. I placed the keys on the counter, turned off the lights in the apartment, and got one last look before locking the door for good.

Eventually, I'd need to look for a second apartment, maybe in the same building, because after all, I did tell Silencer and the crew I had my own place over here. Luckily they haven't suggested coming over yet, but we haven't been hanging that long. Besides, they always working. I have about two weeks before I find another apartment on the side that I won't tell Jackie about. I have to get it when the department wires me some funds through Western Union, like always. I'll get the apartment and find some second-hand stuff to throw in there to make it look like a bachelor pad so the crew feels at home and isn't suspicious if they came over. Jackie had some storage space in her garage that I would put the few furnishings I took along with me. The rest of the items, mainly clothes, would go in the house. She had already prepared a closet for me to hang my clothes in. Her closet in the master bedroom was filled with all her things, but she improvised and took the clothes and shoes in the small closet to a closet in one of the other bedrooms. It always dawned on me that she was this beautiful sistah, staying in a four-bedroom, three-bath house, all alone and not scared. I never really got into a conversation about it, but I did mention it, and she just shrugged it off, saying, "I ain't worried."

I put my clothes on the hangers, arranging my shoes lined neatly on the floor. All settled in now. It was time for me to be nosy. I hate to do it, but my inquisitive side was just taking over. I had to know what secrets she might have. I looked through her drawers and found a vibrator in the top, under some panties. It was big and long and kind of fat. Had a name on the box: Big Black. I didn't think nothing of it. Hell, I masturbate from time to time. Moved on to the bed. Lifting up the mattress, I found a shocking secret, a Glock 9 mm pistol. This is why she wasn't afraid. She had something to make the average burglar shit his pants. It was a pretty gun. Had a sixteen-round clip too. The girl gets better and better. I had to find a way to slip this into a conversation so she could tell me about it. I didn't know how to go about it because I wasn't supposed to be snooping. I know she know; otherwise, she would have hid both Big Black and the gun in a better place. I looked around the rest of the house but didn't find anything.

Two of the other rooms was occupied with furnishings. In one was two computers. The other had a treadmill, a weight set, and some type of ball. I played around with the weights and ran on the treadmill for a couple minutes, something I hadn't done in a long while. It wasn't a surprise that I was completely out of breath after the first minute and a half of running, because I hadn't exercised in months. I could still bench press a good 255 lbs without any hesitation, though. Enough toying around with this stuff. I need to grab a bite to eat. I got a taste for some Mexican food, tamales or enchiladas. I always got some good tamales at a nice little Mexican shack uptown. I don't remember the name, but I know the waiter, Pedro, like he was my brother. He would always seat and serve me whenever I went there to eat. He would always greet me as señor and seat me in the far corner off to myself. The average nigga would take offense to this, thinking they was trying to keep them from being seen eating there, but I liked it. I like being in a quiet setting when I eat out to take my mind off the things going on. I don't know how he knew, but I was glad he did. Pedro would bring me a large lemonade and two tortillas with some sweet butter before my food to keep me occupied before the main course came. I didn't think nothing of the niceness, just thought he was happy to be working in America. I imagine it was far better than in the country he was from. I got my tamales, served with extra cheese on top and some Tobasco sauce to give it that extra zing. I ate and was on my way. I don't know where I was going now, because Jackie wasn't home yet, and I didn't want to go there to be alone. I guess I will go over to check out Silencer and the boys.

I pulled up to the complex parking lot and parked in one of the empty spots. It was a cold night. Late November is always cold, so again, they were all inside. I rang the doorbell and was buzzed up after yelling my name into the intercom at the top of my lungs, thirteen stories up. It was Do-Dirt who looked out the window to verify my identity. After walking up all thirteen flights, the apartments was filled with regulars, with the exception of a thick sistah I had never seen before. I got some dap from everyone in the house and a gentle "What up?" from the sistah. After the what-ups, I got teased about leaving the other night too early. They told me I missed a good switcharoo party. A switcharoo party was when the girls switched fuck partners from the original ones they fucked. I asked what happened to the girl I was with. Since there was nobody for her, lucky Silencer got two girls was the answer.

The spot was booming tonight. The doorbell was buzzing nonstop. After about ten customers, Silencer relieved Scooby of his serving duties and called me up in just that fashion. "Rookie, you up. If you want to be down, you going to have to put in work."

I was never so glad. Things was going better than I hoped. I didn't have to ask to be put down. I was chosen. Not only was this a sign of friendship. It was a sign of trust. I was given a paper bag of twenty-dollar rocks to serve. I don't know how much total was in the bag, but it was a lot. I was showed how the spot was operated from Scooby. The customers rang the doorbell. The looker on duty verified identity, the server buzzed them up, the money was transferred in an adjacent apartment, and the server served them. It was smooth. The set up was confusing like that so the customers could not pinpoint who served them. That way, in the case of a raid, the police would have no proof or an exact buy. In other words, no case. I did it under watch a couple of times, and then I was on my own. The bag was going down pretty fast. I was almost out an hour into getting it. Silencer checked on the bag size. Seeing that it was nearly empty, he brought out another full bag from under the sofa. It was kept on the table until the current bag was completely sold out, I guess to keep track of how much was sold. He must have had been the bagger and knew how much was in each bag, so when it came time to count the money he knew how much was supposed to be made from each color-coded bag. During a break in the action, Silencer asked if I liked what I was doing and if I wanted to be a full-time worker in his crew. I quickly said, "Hell yeah, without a doubt." He asked about my other job and mentioned some shit about not being able to make the kind of money there that I could make with him. I agreed and told him I got fired anyway. Ran him the story about fucking a girl too long, went in late, and the boss fired my ass. He laughed just like the employee did when I told him.

I was to make fifteen hundred a week, starting out as a server, and would have to work my way up in rank and in pay. I guess this was my official initiation into the crew. I now had to think of a way I was going to spend time with Jackie and be down with the crew. I needed to stay tight with Silencer because that was my ticket to bigger fish, but I also needed to keep Jackie without getting her suspicious of my new hobby. She said she would work on getting me a job. How could I tell her I'd become a drug dealer? Furthermore, how could I ever tell her the real, which was I am an undercover agent?

This shit is getting too deep, but I can handle it. After all, my name is Incognito, and this is what I live for.

I called Jackie on my cell phone from the spot to tell her I would be coming a little later after realizing it had gotten late and she hadn't called me since earlier. I didn't know how the fellas was going to act about me checking in, so I kept the conversation short. Told her I was hanging with some friends and would be over around one to break her off. I had to make it seem as if I were just fucking her to throw them off a good way to make up an excuse if they asked to go over with me one day. I would eventually have to let them come over once so they could feel I was really down and trusted them as they trusted me. After hanging up, just as I expected, someone said something. Do-Dirt made a comment about me having to check in. I told him I was just making sure her mama was gone before I come over so I could get some. I said her mama didn't like me, so I don't go over when she home. He just laughed and said, "Whatever." I was cool for the rest of the time there.

After we sold out of the last bag, we went to get something to eat to cure the appetite from the weed high we had. It was a gyro shop on the corner that stayed open twenty-four hours. I never been there before, but they seemed to go there often, considering they don't leave out of the buildings regularly. The shack was operated by some Arabs. Explains the reason it being open twenty-four hours. Every food shop they have in the hood be open around the clock, and be the same workers there too. It be like they vampires, but the hustlers be serving around the clock, so I guess it go hand in hand. We ordered a nine-piece bucket of chicken, three gyros, three sodas, and a milkshake. The milkshake was for me because I didn't drink soda.

Eating the food sparked some general conversation. Since they already knew where I used to live, I asked them where they lived. Silencer lived in Cornell, Do-Dirt lived in Cornell, Red lived in Cornell, and Scooby lived on David St. When I heard that, I got excited inside. Thought he was going to say the cross street, Crescent, but instead, he said Sixty-Third, a long way from Crescent—in fact, the other side of town. I thought, *What the fuck this kid doing down in the projects when he lived in a well-to-do suburb*? I wondered if his parents knew he was hanging down here, so I asked.

"Hey, Scooby, what the fuck you down here for if you live in the suburbs?"

"Ain't shit to do up there. Plus, my pops be tripping. Beating my ass and shit just for talking on the phone or eating. So I left home." Damn, he be tripping like that. That's some fucked-up shit. "I been staying down here with this broad I know from the doctor office I used to go to. She a vet."

A vet is an older woman with experience in fucking, usually over twenty-five. Scooby was only eighteen.

"That's cool. She be breaking you off?"

"Hell, yeah! We smoke a blunt and she be ready. I get chewed and screwed."

"Your ass a fool. I ain't mad at you."

The conversation went on pretty much about nothing for the next fifteen minutes or so, until we got up to leave. We dropped Scooby off at his crib and went back to the projects. I gave some dap and got in my car to head home.

I knew I was going to have to get my apartment back in case we had other nights like this and they decided to come over. I had enough for the rent, but I would need the security deposit. Maybe I could get it from Jackie. I didn't know what I could tell her it was for, though. I thought a little bit longer, and it came to me. I'll tell her I need it for a credit-card bill. Luckily I had the bogus one the bureau gave me.

I got in the house at 2:47 am. Jackie was sleeping on the couch. She must have fell asleep waiting for me because the TV was still on. I turned it off and woke her up by telling her lets go to bed. I could tell she was glad I came because she was smiling and holding on to me walking back to the bedroom. She was already wearing her pajamas, a T-shirt with no bra or panties. I was aroused from looking at the bottom part of her ass peeking out of the T-shirt. While she lay in the bed, I got undressed so I could warm up while laying next her so we could fall to sleep. I was out before you knew it.

In the morning, before she left for work, I asked for the money in a way so it didn't look like I was begging. I said, "Jackie do you think you could loan me $1,500 so I could pay my credit card bill? I'll pay you back once I get a new job."

She told me, "You don't have to borrow it. I'll give it to you."

I was more than happy, expressing it by saying, "Thank you" before holding her and giving her a long, wet kiss. She left for work while I was in the shower. When I got out, I seen the money and a note on the nightstand. The note read, *Michael, I really do enjoy your company. You have touched my heart. I hope I make you feel good and that this doesn't end, for I have never had anyone as good as you. Love, Jackie.* After I read the, note I began to feel sad. I knew this would have to end and I would feel sorry for Jackie being hurt. There would be no possible way I could stay with her. Oh well, I can't worry about that now. I need to focus on getting the apartment. I'll call Mrs. Holland in the car. I'm sure she'll be glad to hear I want the apartment back. I just hope one is still available.

"Hello, Mrs. Holland. This is Michael, your former tenant in apartment 101. How are you doing?"

"I'm fine and you?"

"I'm doing good. Do you have any one-bedroom apartments available left?"

"I don't know. Why, she kicked you out already? That wasn't even three months."

"No I'm just looking for somewhere I can chill when I want to be alone."

"I got the same apartment you was in before, just painted too. When you want it?"

"I want it right away. Can you meet me over there in about a hour to give me the keys?"

"You got the rent and security deposit?"

"Yes I got all that."

"I'll meet you over there. If I'm not there when you get there, just wait in the front. I won't be much longer."

"Okay, Mrs. Holland. See you then. Thanks."

I was never more happy than now. She a life saver. I opened another can of worms. I know this means I more than likely will have to get sexual with her again. That's cool, though. Only this time, I'm going to have to get some head or get my penis wet. I better stop at the gas station before I go over there. Otherwise, I might not make it. This motherfucker on empty.

Please, God, let me make it to the gas station. I would hate to have to push it. This is too heavy for me to be pushing and trying to steer. I got six blocks to go. Come on, light. Turn green.

I kept one foot on the brake and the other one pumping the accelerator so the car could stay idling in order not to shut off. I learned that from a shade-tree mechanic while working undercover on a different case. I made it to the pump in the knick of time it shut off just as I got in front of the pump. Damn, I'm glad today going be a good day. It started out right. I got the money from Jackie, got the apartment back, and now I made it to the gas station without having to push. I went inside to pay for the gas—twelve dollars on regular. I grabbed some chips and a juice while I was in there too.

While I was pumping the gas, a police car pulled in the lot behind this nice-ass Lexus. It was shiny black with some chrome rims and black tint. The dude that got out was in suit and tie, must be some professional-type cat. He don't have nothing to worry about, but I still bet he was nervous. Nervous cause the law was behind him. Hell, I even get nervous sometime, and I *am* the law. It is just natural instinct for a black man when they see the police behind them. It is not so bad now for me, though. They didn't fuck with him, just went in the station too. They must don't have nothing to do if they just riding behind niggas, following them in gas stations and shit.

As I was getting in the car after pumping my gas, I seen the boys get in they squad. I was waiting for the traffic to ease so I could pull out, hoping they don't get behind me and pull me over, for I still had a half a blunt in the ash tray. They turned out and went in the other direction, not paying me no attention. I could now go hang out with the fellas, see what they up to, not that I don't already know, but who knows? Today they might decide not to sell drugs or smoke. Yeah right. Who I'm talking about?

I pulled in the back parking lot of Cornell, parked in an open spot two rows from the building we occupied. I took the half blunt with me so we could light it up, help start the day off right with them. It was cold outside, so it wasn't nobody outside except for customers. They always out. Even if it's twenty below, you going to see one or more of them out. In the hallway, I ran into Shelly. She stopped me on the way to the second flight of stairs.

"Why you didn't call me yet?" she asked.

"I don't know. I don't know what happened to your number. I looked everywhere for it. Still couldn't find it. Sorry."

"I bet. If you don't want to fuck with me, just tell me. I ain't going to trip just because we fucked. I wanted to fuck anyway—shit."

"No, it ain't even like that, boo. I just lost the number. Why don't you go write it down and bring it to the spot so we could finish smoking this blunt, alright?"

"Okay, I'm going to get Tracy and Tanisha to come with me."

"Cool, I'll let Do-Dirt and Red know. Holler."

I'm tired as hell walking up these punk-ass flights of stairs. This some bullshit. This motherfucker need a working elevator. Now at the door, I knocked three times to get in, to be greeted by Red.

"What up, nigga?"

"Chillin, Do-Dirt."

"What it do baby?"

"What it always."

Silencer said, "Let me smash some of those chips since you didn't bring enough."

"Knock yo-self out, playboy."

I wasn't even thinking about it. I was just trying to get out of there before five-o started sweating. They had already followed some nigga in there. You know how they be sweating.

"Yeah, Shelly said her, Tracy, and Tanisha coming down here in a minute. They want to smoke. Here, got something to get started, something I was smoking on last night.

"Give it here," Red hollered as he put the game on pause. Him and Do-Dirt was playing Madden football. I lit the blunt and took two hits before I passed it. I took a seat on the couch and watched them play while talking to Silencer. He threw a sack to roll up. I was much obliged. I rolled up three stuffed blunts perfectly. They were tightly rolled in a strawberry wrap, filled with Indo, some of the best regular weed you can find. As I lit one of the stuffies, Silencer began to philosophize, which he always did when we were just chilling, smoking weed. He got to talking about relationships—how women be manipulating men. His theory is that women say they want a man that's going to be there for them, that they be romantic and sensitive, but when you ain't like that, they be cool until they get you. I asked him to break it down for me.

"Okay, check it. Y'all be doing all type of shit at first—you know, going to the movies, out to eat, and just straight fucking, right? But then, when you tell her you love her, she change."

I asked, "What you mean she change?"

"She start wanting you to be in the house all early and shit. She want you to cuddle, hold her. She start checking your phone, calling back numbers. Just doing all type of crazy shit."

"Yeah you right a little bit."

"Nigga, I'm right all the way. Why you think I just fuck thug bitches or jump-downs."

"Why?"

"Because they don't ask for all that. They just want to smoke and fuck. Plus, you take them to Red Lobster or Denny's, they cool."

"You crazy as fuck, dog, but if it work for you, that's cool. I do think you right—them thug bitches and jump-downs do be freaks though."

Red and Do-Dirt shouted, "Hell, yeah. Anyway where Shelly and them at?"

"I don't know. They supposed to be here. You got the number? I'll call."

"He called out the number in between puffs on the second blunt. Just as I was dialing the number, there was a knock on the door.

I answered, "Who is it?"

Tanisha yelled, "Your baby mama. Now open the door."

"So, you got jokes, huh?"

"You know I love you, boo."

They all give they what up's and have a seat.

"You getting your ass kicked, Do-Dirt?" goes Shelly.

"You crazy in your head. Can't nobody mess with me in this game. I be whippin' motherfuckers ninety going north."

She replied, "Okay, I feel you, stunna. Do the damn thang."

Tracy goes, "Who turn is it on the blunt? Smell like some killa."

"It's still my turn," came from Silencer. "Light that one up. Y'all came at the right time. We was just talking about how women be changing when they know they got a nigga."

"What you mean?" said Tanisha.

"You know, how when she think she got him whipped, she be making him come home all early, stop hanging with his boys, checking his pockets, and checking his phone. What's up with that? Who got an answer for us?"

"That be them insecure bitches be doing that shit. Hell, as long as the nigga know where home is and don't bring me home no diseases, I'm cool," answers Tanisha.

"That's what I'm talking about," goes in Shelly.

Tracy, on the other hand, got to talking about how she do expect a man not to have a problem with her checking his pockets or phone. She explained that she don't care about him hanging with his boys or even fucking other hoes—just be real with her when she ask him about stuff, especially when it come to the fucking other hoes, cause she might want to fuck the hoe too. When she said that, Do-Dirt, Silencer, Red, and me was stunned. We all looked in amazement, quiet as hell. We was surprised that she liked girls too. I guess Shelly and Tanisha already knew, because they didn't even blink.

Silencer asked, "What you mean you might want to fuck too?"

She answered, "Just what I said. I might want to fuck the bitch too. Sometime I don't want no penis. A bitch got to get her vagina ate the right way."

We all bust out in laughter. The girls all gave each other a high five. Shelly said, "I know that shit right. Y'all niggas be acting like y'all don't do it. But I never went that way. I just wait for the nigga to do it. I don't know about that bumping coochies shit."

Tracy hit the blunt, saying, "I told y'all, don't knock it until you try it."

Do-Dirt beat Red 21 to 8 in the game, which Red blamed on the controller.

We was all just sitting there now quiet until Red put on some music. He threw on some classic shit. I hadn't heard the shit in a long time. It was that N.W.A., Niggaz Wit Attitudes. I remember playing that shit when it first came out almost everyday. As we was listening to the sounds of "I Rather Fuck You," the room became quiet. We was all in a daze. The already dimly lit room was full of Indo smoke. Time flew by. It was just after 1:30 p.m. when I got there, but it was now a little past 6:00. After the track went off, Shelly suggested we go to the hotel to get away and relax. She wanted to go to the hotel over in Riverbrook, the suburbs where all the white people live. I knew where it was but never been, because I had no reason to, just got briefed by the department that Darius frequents there with different girls. Silencer agreed with her to go so we could get in the pool they had. He told them to go get some stuff to wear because we going to spend the night in one of the suites. Red had Tracy, Silencer had Tanisha, and I had Shelly, so that left Do-Dirt out, cause the girl that was with them last time couldn't find no babysitter—that's why she wasn't in the spot with us.

When we got to the bottom of the stairs, just before the front door, Silencer came up with a plan that we was going to try to get them to have sex with each other before we fuck, just to make things exciting. The rest of us agreed to the plan. What man wouldn't want to watch two women—maybe three—have sex with each other? We went to the truck to wait on the ladies because they was taking too long. Silencer decided to drive his Suburban. I knew it was nice, but I didn't know it was *this* nice. I mean I had seen the outside, with its candy-apple-red pearl paint, shiny chrome rims, and tinted windows, but the inside was even better. The inside was peanut butter brown. It had plush leather seats, built-in TV and DVD player, four twelve-inch kickers, and surround sound. This was better than most people home theater system. I complimented him by saying, "Silencer, this shit tight than a bitch."

He nodded and thanked me. "You stay with us, work yo way up, you could have one of these too, dog."

I replied, "That's what I'm talking about."

Shelly and her girls was coming now. When they got in the truck, Do-Dirt asked if they had a buddy that can come for him. Tracy had said she did, a girl that lived on the other end of town that would be down to come.

"Let me call her." She called asked for Erica. "Hey, what's up girl? What you doing? You down to get out. Me, Shelly and few fellas going to go to the hotel to smoke and chill in a suite. We on our way to get you. Be ready. Let's go get her. She stay on Eighty-Third and Taylor. Just make a left when you get there."

Silencer hit the expressway to cut some time so we could hurry up to the hotel to get a suite booked. After a ten-minute drive, we made it to Erica's house, which was in the lower section of the city.

This was the true definition of ghetto. There were rundown houses—shacks, to be exact. Erica's house sat on the corner next to a hole-in-the-wall bar, which looked like a front for the numerous men and boys hanging in front of it. From past experience, I could safely say they were dealers, aligned by rank. Erica came out of the house wearing skin-tight jeans, a button-up blouse, and a bandana wrapped around her head as if it were a headband. As she was walking to the truck, we heard the soldiers harassing her. They were screaming things like, "Who you going to do now?" "Can I get some later?" and so on. I would bet any money that all of them had fucked her. She hopped in the truck, dapping Tracy and Shelly, then kindly acknowledging the rest of us. As we drove off, the girls began to talk while we listened the sounds of Big Mike.

After driving for a while, Erica must have got the scoop on who she was going be kicking it with, because she switched seats with Tracy to sit by Do-Dirt. They began talking—I guess to get to know each other a little bit from the looks of it. They was connecting, because Do-Dirt had her laughing.

Before we got to the hotel, my cell phone vibrated in my pocket. It was Jackie. I didn't want to answer it in front of the girls because I didn't want her to hear them in the background, since then I would have to explain what I was doing. I answered and put my finger over the part where you talk to filter out the noise and took it off when it was my turn to talk. Jackie asked where I was at, since she hadn't seen me since earlier today. I couldn't tell the truth, so I quickly came up with a lie. I told her I was with a few of the guys I met at work while working at the factory. I also didn't want Shelly or the guys drilling me about who I was talking to, so I hurriedly told her we was driving to Minnesota to look at this truck one of them wanted to buy. She asked when I would be back. I told her as soon as we got done, but we might decide to go out to a club while we there. If so, I'd be back in the morning. If so, I'd call to let her know.

She said, "Okay, baby, just call me to let me know. Love you."

I was glad she didn't want to talk long because we was at the hotel now and everybody would've been able to hear our conversation. Shelly had to get the suite because she had a Visa card. By the look on the front desk clerk face, you would think he didn't want to give us the room. That's how it was out in the boonies/ suburbs. When a lot of black people come, they either get scared or prejudiced on you. We got the room on the fifth floor, one that had a Jacuzzi in the room and two king-size beds. The pool was on the bottom level by the gym and rec room. We got settled in the room and dressed for the pool. Down in the pool it was empty, so we had it all to ourselves, but we had to be respectful; we couldn't get too loud or do any crazy stuff. We swam a little bit and just chilled out, talking and playing truth or dare. Some of the dares was to kiss somebody or show some nakedness, and some of the truth was to tell something about the craziest or freakiest shit you did. This was a great icebreaker for everybody to lead up to what would take place upstairs—especially for Erica, since most had never met her. Speaking of which, she did some freaky shit, like fucking two dudes at the same time.

It was getting late, so we had to head up to the room, cause the pool area was about the be off-limits. We got up to the room and raided the bar and fridge to cure our appetite that always come after you get done swimming. Now it was time for the showdown to take place, hopefully. Silencer asked the question, "Y'all going to freak each other while we watch?"

Tracy was down, but the others didn't want to participate. After trying to persuade them to get it on with each other, it was still a no-go, so we turned out the lights and did our individual thing.

4

A week had passed since the night I stayed out with the crew, and Jackie hadn't said anything about it, which I didn't really understand, but was glad. Had that been Marcy, I would have been on the couch. It was a cold, sunny Sunday morning. Jackie decided she wanted to go to church this morning to get some soul-cleansing. I thought it was a good idea too, since I couldn't remember the last time I stepped foot in a church. It's not because I don't believe in God or religion, but the preachers always made it last too long. They stand in the front of the pulpit, talk a little about the Scriptures from the Bible, and then spend a lot more time talking about what sins the congregation are committing, not including themselves. After it goes on for a hour or two, they ask for your money. I just don't get it.

We took our shower together and got in a quick round of fucking before we got dressed and headed out the door. Jackie was Catholic, so we went to her Catholic church. The church was older, with early Roman architectural designs on the outside. The inside was beautifully shaped, with high arched ceilings, cherry oak trimmings around the walls, and different depictions of the Virgin Mary. Being Methodist, I had never been to a Catholic church. This was all new to me. I remember going to church as a youngster. Service would last a long time. I hope this didn't. Everyone made their way to the altar to pray with their rosaries before taking seats in the pews. The priest rose out of his seat, as everyone was now seated. He preached a sermon about demons and angels taking souls daily, saying a couple of hymns, took the collection, gave out Communion, and then the service was over.

Heading out the cathedral, Jackie spoke to many members I'm guessing she hadn't seen for sometime, because the time she spent chatting was longer than the sermon. I guess that is a woman thing. Finally we were leaving. I was all too glad. Not that I don't like to give praise or being around churchfolk, but I didn't want anyone to see me that might,remember, mentioning it at an inopportune moment like if I was with the crew. If that happened, man, I would for sure be a goner. They would for sure think I'm weak. Worse, my cover could be blown. In the car, Jackie asked me how I liked the service. Now, I didn't want to tell her I didn't like it, because that would probably hurt her feelings, but if I lied, she would for sure ask me to go again. I decided to tell a half-truth with a lie on top of it. I said it was nice but I just couldn't understand the message. I'd better get the whole Catholic thing if I were raised in it. Jackie nodded her head, saying, "All right, baby. I'm just glad you came. I won't pressure to keep coming." I replied back with a promise that I would come again, just might be a minute.

We were riding along listening to some gospel music station in between short talks, and it dawned on me that I really didn't know much about her job, so I asked the name of the company she worked for. She replied, "Power Broker, Inc."

"What type of company is that?"

"It's an investment firm."

She was responsible for the Eastern District's holdings of the company, which spanned from Kentucky to Rhode Island. Her work consisted of keeping records of the earnings and losses of the satellite sites spanning those states. She also looked at financial records of possible merger companies. We next talked about what to do now, since it was just after eleven in the morning. It was a cold day out. Old Man Winter was finally settling in. That eliminated going to the park for a walk. She came up with the idea to go to the zoo.

It was a good idea. I hadn't been to the zoo since the kids were in second grade. Always willing to see something new. We drove to the zoo, taking the scenic route. Jackie lived in a nice house in a nice neighborhood, but the route we took was spectacular. The houses were huge, with nicely kept lawns and trees. Some even had waterfall decorative in the front. The road stretched for blocks—at least two miles—before descending into a more modest looking neighborhood.

After a few turns and stoplights, we were at the zoo. After parking, as we walked up to the pay gate, Jackie mentioned how she would love to have a house like that one day after she got married. She said it would be good to raise a family and throw nice, sophisticated parties. I agreed with her as we stood in the long line to enter. Looks like more people had the same idea. It was mostly white people in line. Family-event type shit, it looked like. It didn't take long to get to the entrance to get our admission ticket. It was $18.50 for the both of us.

Inside was nice. There were different sections with various attractions. We started with the aquariums. The building with the aquariums was in had at least fifty different tanks, each with different species. There was freshwater tanks and saltwater tanks, both filled with imitation coral reefs and savvy swimmers. The saltwater tanks had the more colorful of the two. There were yellow with black stripes, orange with white stripes, even purple. Looking at these was a true testament to God's creation. You had the same creatures yet completely different, I guess because they came from different parts of the world, kind of like humans.

We finished looking at the fish and made our way to the reptiles. Jackie wasn't as into the reptiles as she was the fish; by the way she was squirming, you could tell they gave her the creeps. I, on the other hand, liked the different amphibians. There were the big-eyed frogs, the dinosaur-like iguanas, and slivery snakes and lizards. It was great. They were kept in tanks like the fish, but these were heated tanks. The heat lamps that were at the top of them kept the tanks warm. This was next to the monkeys and other mammals.

There were gorillas, chimps, pandas, and of course monkeys. The enclosure they were in was arranged to resemble their own natural environment. Each enclosure had trees and grass. Some of the mammals were up close to the glass. Others were sitting up high in the trees or hiding afar.

We now made our way out to the outside animals—first stop: polar bears. There were two polar bears sharing one cold watery manmade pond, alongside a manmade cave. The polar bears were swimming away in the water, not paying attention to onlookers, who were snapping pictures, looking on in amazement. Making our rounds, we wound up at the seals. They were busy feeding on fish, except for a baby, which was more focused on the small crowd surrounding the lining of the fence that separated them.

It was now the end of our tour. With nowhere to go, we got in the car and decided to have lunch. It wasn't nowhere fancy, just a quick lunch at IHOP. Yep, we wanted some good ol' fashioned pancakes, eggs, and sausage, topped off with a nice glass of orange juice. During lunch, Jackie stated she hadn't taken a trip in quite some time and had to use her vacation time before the end of the year or she would lose it. I asked her if she took a vacation where she would go. Her response was Brazil or Puerto Rico. She then said something I didn't expect: "Let's book a cruise tonight so we can go." I was so shocked. I said yes, being caught off guard. I couldn't say anything else. It made her all too happy. We paid for our food and headed to the house. Once there, Jackie immediately got on the computer, searching for the best deals for cruises to our destination. I was busy watching the Bears beat up on the Green Bay Packers, one of the longest rivalries in football. The score was 14 to 7, with the Bears in scoring position on the Green Bay 15-yard line. It was an exciting game. The fans were really into it. The announcers were dramatic, as if it were a playoff game. It was third and two. The bears rushed to get set back two inches back—a bad attempt going up against the Packers big offensive line. As the players were lining up to go for the field goal, they decided to go for the touchdown. It was a fake end around. The running back made it to the four-yard line to get tackled and stopped in his tracks.

Now Jackie was calling me to her, I guess to look at some of the deals to get my opinion on which ones would be better for us. When I saw the prices, I considered how I was going to contribute. I only had $3,500 in the account the bureau set up for me, but that was not to be touched for personal use, only to help with the case. I didn't have any of my personal bank account information or even any of my real identification, so I couldn't withdraw any money from that account. I did have some of the money Silencer was paying me for working the spot, though. I could use that if needed to, although I was trying to save that as well to use later.

I'll wait to see if she asks me. For now, I'll just look along with her, giving my opinion.

We looked at some that were cheap to really expensive. I guessed that the rates were based on which airline and cruise ship you chose, along with the nights and days you wanted to stay. The best deal we came up with was a seven-night, six-day cruise, which departed from Miami going to Saint Lucia in the Bahamas. We would have to catch a flight from Milwaukee to Miami aboard Delta Airlines. The total package, for the both of us, was $2,700. The dates we were to be going were January 16 through January 24. After booking the vacation, I asked Jackie if she'd be able to get vacation time on such short notice. She replied, "I got clout like that."

We finished the rest of the night packing and relaxing, watching television. We cuddled in the bed before falling asleep midway through the *Good Times* marathon.

The next morning, Jackie woke up earlier than usual—I guess to make sure everything was going to be taken care of. She had to go to her mother's house to make sure she would check on the house and water her plants. She also had to get her hair done. Before we could leave, she had to make a stop at her office to give a rundown on the numbers for her boss. Finally, she had to get a couple of bathing suits and outfits for the island.

I was showered and ready to go by noon. I was glad I had a fake passport given to me by the bureau. She was to be back at two. I was excited to go. I had never been to the Bahamas, or anywhere else outside the States. Jackie didn't ask me to pay for anything, which I was glad for, but I did want to help pay for something, so after I was dressed, I went to get a little of the money I had at the apartment. That way, I could at least pay for some of the things on the ship and island, like flowers and souvenirs. I took $700 of the $3,900 I had stashed under the carpet in the closet to help show her half a good time. I made it back to her house with a little time to kill. It was just 1:16, so I sat listening to some music. I had one of my favorite CDs playing: Guns N' Roses, *Appetite for Destruction*, on the stereo. I got through the whole CD and halfway through another CD that Jackie had in the player before she made it back a little after three. She arrived with our tickets, her outfits, some outfits for me, and beads that were to go around our neck like a necklace. We didn't have much time because our flight was to leave at 5:30. We hurriedly got together our things, locked up the house, and headed for the airport. We had to hurry because the freeway was going to be crowded. It was rush hour, which meant all the people were leaving downtown and heading home from work. We made it to the airport with forty-five minutes to park the car, check in our luggage, and get to the gate. We devised a plan that I was to check in the luggage while she went to park the car so we could meet at the gate. The plan worked to perfection. We made it to the gate with little time to kill, as Jackie was running up just as the plane was boarding. The flight to Miami from Milwaukee was two hours and thirty minutes, nonstop.

The flight went smoothly, except for some minor turbulence flying over Atlanta. We touched down at the Miami airport with 80-degree temperature awaiting us. The moon was shining brightly in the sky, with no clouds. We had to find a hotel to stay at for the night because the ship wasn't set to depart until the following day. We stayed at the Excel Inn, which was located ten minutes from the departure site. After checking in, we decided to go out and see some of Miami, since neither one of us had been there. We took the tourist attraction and nightlife magazine that was already in the room as a helpful tool in figuring out what to do. The hotel was located in what appeared to be a decent area, but you really couldn't tell what was around the corners, as I learned in Milwaukee. After walking the area and eating at one of the Cuban restaurants, we made our way back to the hotel to get some sleep.

The next morning, while boarding the ship, we ran into one of Jackie's childhood friends, Wendy, along with her husband. She and Jackie talked for a while before both of them introduced us men into the picture. Jackie introduced me as her boyfriend. Then Wendy introduced William. After the small talk and introductions, we parted ways, with the girls saying they'd hook up later to catch up on old times. Our cabin was on the middle deck near the center of the ship, which was quiet, as it was far from the engines. Boarding took almost two hours, as there were nearly two hundred people aboard. We finally left the port a little past noon, set for the Bahamas. There was a lot of entertainment on the ship, something for everyone—or at least almost everyone. You always have those that are never satisfied. There was gambling, a live band, swimming, movies, dancing, even exercise. We wanted to make the best of the vacation by doing as much as possible. After securing everything in the cabin, we went up to the deck to check out the scenery from the open ocean. The Miami skyline was great, including all the beachfront houses that lined the shore. We walked to the bar to get something refreshing to drink. It was still early, so we didn't want to get anything too heavy that would get us drunk, so we ordered two raspberry margaritas. The bartender made them to perfection—just the right amount of alcohol and the perfect blend of fruits. Sitting at the bar, we started talking about how we had met and what went through our minds the moment we saw each other. I said when I first seen her walking up to the line, I thought she was one of the most beautiful women I had ever seen. I also told her how I thought about what it would be like fucking her. It was funny, because excluding the part about me being the most beautiful man she had ever seen, she thought the same thing. She said, "I thought about what I was going to do when we fucked, because I knew I was going to fuck you when you said hi."

"How you knew that?"

"It's just a woman's instinct, baby, or at least mine anyway. I mean, it is not too often that I do it, but when I do run across somebody that look good and I get that vibe from them, I'll make it happen. Now that I got you, I don't have to worry about that no more. Besides, I know that was dangerous even though we did use protection."

She gave me a kiss. Finishing our drink, we ordered another to enhance the conversation, as it was getting good talking now about the ladies she was there with that night. She began telling me about how one of them had been one of her friends since childhood. They had met at gym class while in middle school and been friends ever since. One of the other ladies worked in the office with her. They go out together occasionally because her husband be tripping. Plus, she got four kids. The last lady was somebody they met at the hair shop. She didn't really like her because she be phony, always bragging on what she got, how she could have any man she want, shit like that. You know, high school stuff. I agreed with her on that shit. We moved on to check out what was going on at the gambling scene, as we wanted some excitement. Neither of us was into gambling, but from what you see on TV, when people be gambling, winning or losing, they be screaming either way. We stopped at the craps table, checking out how it worked. We seen the roller who rolled the dice and the side betters who placed bets on what the roller would roll. It all seemed risky to me, but I guess it was either luck or statistical strategy on winning. As I was watching, I counted how many times different pairs and numbers appeared on each roll. I figured the best bet was to put money on a six or eight, since they came up the most. Jackie got into it, so we lined up to roll. Even though it was risky, betting the minimum $10 each roll, she did it. While she rolled, I was placing bets on six or eight. The first roll came out a ten. People then placed their bets. She rolled four more rolls before rolling another ten. She didn't believe it when she won, doubling her money. She didn't stop. She kept on rolling some twenty more rolls, winning all of them. Our total winnings, with her rolling and my betting, was $650. That was a lot of excitement. She said she wanted to do everything, so we continued the excitement. We passed the blackjack table. Looked like it was too complicated and boring, so we moved on to the roulette table. I had seen this played before but didn't understand how people could bet their money on a little ball spinning around a wheel, waiting to stop on a colored number. We didn't play this game either. Jackie decided to keep the winnings and head to the cabin.

We relaxed in the cabin for a short time, just holding each other and talking. Soon, Jackie began touching and feeling, even kissing me on the neck, down my chest and stomach, then on the head of my penis. I was instantly aroused, wanting to take her. As she put the head of my penis all the way in her mouth, she began sucking it in and out until I was fully erect. I immediately pulled off my shirt as she took off her blouse and bra. I brought her up to face level to give her a kiss and feel the warmth of her firm breasts against my bare chest. While removing the bottom half of our clothes, she asked me if I wanted to play a game. I asked what kind of game. She said, "I do whatever you do." I knew what it sound like, but had never played, so to be sure, I asked how to play. She said, "You know, if you do something, I get to do it, or if I do something, you get to do it." I replied okay. How bad could it be. It actually sounded like fun, since our sex was always good. She started it out by biting my nipples, which felt really good. I never had that done before. She circled them with her tongue, sucking them and biting them. Now it was my turn. I gently caressed her tits with my hands, placing her nipples in my mouth one at a time, then both at the same time. As she was feeling the effect, they became hard, so I bit them with just the right amount of pressure, which sent her head back before she sighed a gentle moan. She pushed me down on the bed and went down to my manhood, stroking it with her hand before placing it in her mouth. She went up and down with her full lips while licking the tip with it still in her mouth. This was a great feeling—it was like she was a different person than I had previously screwed. She did this for few minutes, including stroking my balls and the area between my asshole and balls. This was now feeling really good, which made me sigh a gentle moan. I almost put my legs in the air. As she came back up, she pushed my head down to her clean-shaved lovebox. I quickly tasted the sweetness of the cream that had already secreted from the effects of the foreplay we were engaged in. I slid my tongue up and down her vagina, sticking it in the hole, going in circles, then began to lick her clitoris, fierce but gentle. She was grabbing my head, moaning and gyrating her body before having the first of many orgasms that evening. After putting me on my back to hop on and ride me, she got on all fours to take it from the back. I pounded her with long, hard thrusts, which made her say my name and a whole lot of other sex talk. She then told me to put it in her ass, which now I was glad to do. I never had the chance to do it, but I always wanted to. I never had any thoughts of doing any homosexual stuff, like being with a man, but from watching porno movies, I seen how the women responded to that. I put it in her ass, as instructed. She told me to take it slow at first, to get it to open up, then pound her. I felt it tight as I went in. Then it got wet and opened up. As I was pounding, she began screaming my name and a lot of other sex talk, which almost made me cum instantly. Getting ready to cum, I started going faster, sending her into a frenzy of moans. She had to bite the pillow to keep it down. She sent out three multiple nuts as I came all over her ass. With a grin on her face, she said, "Thank you, baby. Now it's my turn." I looked in confusion as I remembered we were playing "Whatever you do, I do." I was kind of puzzled, because I didn't know exactly how she was going to screw me in the ass without a penis. Then, out of the bottom drawer, she pulled out a strap-on dildo. I now began to get a little scared, cause my asshole was about to get entered. I didn't want to feel like I was gay. I did stick my finger in it occasionally while taking showers, which felt kind of good, but that was it. I manned up, bending over to fulfill the promise I had made like a man. It hurt going in, but as she eased it in further, with each thrust, it began to feel good. I now became aroused by the penetration, instantly becoming erect again. As she kept pumping in and out, she began to have a massive orgasm. To my amazement, I did too. After the ordeal, we lay in the bed, cuddling each other. I asked whether she thought that made me gay. She replied, "Of course not—as long as you don't do it with a man." I told her she didn't have to worry about that but she had better not tell nobody about this. She said in a smirking manner, "I keep what we do between us. I hope you do too. I hope we can do it again with your freaky ass." We took a shower together to get dressed for the night of dancing we were about to do.

Out on the deck, we ran into Wendy and William, who had already been dancing. Wendy asked us to join them for the evening if we didn't have plans. We agreed to spend the evening with them. We began the evening with dinner. The dining area was nice. It was dimly lit, with burning candles in the center of every table. The tables were lined with white cloths and maroon lap napkins. There was a full-course menu, with appetizers, extravagant desserts, and a variety of main dishes. I decided to have the chef's special: a filleted Alaskan salmon over rice pilaf, served with a glass of red wine. Jackie ordered baked chicken with scallops, and William ordered the same thing for himself and Wendy, shrimp Alfredo, without her having a say in the matter. They were kind of weird. It was as if she let him think for her and speak for her. During the conversation over the dinner, he rambled on about how good of a lawyer he was, how he had made partner in his firm in just under three years, and how he graduated at the top of his class in his Ivy League school. This was the most boring motherfucker I had ever met. I could only imagine what Wendy was thinking. I bet when they having sex, he counts the minutes it takes them to climax—if Wendy even gets to that point.

As the evening went on, our dinner complete and dessert on its way, William finally got quiet. Jackie and Wendy began talking as William asked me questions about my life. He wanted to know what I did for a living. I lied, telling him I was a factory worker (technically I was as Incognito). He got to asking me whether I graduated high school, how my childhood was growing up, whether I had two parents in the home, and a bunch of other idiotic bullshit.

I was glad to hear the ladies ask if we were ready to go dance. There were two dance areas, one with hip club music, the other with classical ballroom music. We first went to the ballroom hall, the kind of stuff William lived for. This was a new experience for Jackie and me both, but we made the best of it. The routine was simple—just walk in circles while slow dancing. Even sounds boring. We danced through ten minutes of piano playing, then headed for the crunk music dance area. This was the twenty-something crowd, the hype people, although there were some older gals and gents in the room. Everyone was grooving to the beat, having a good time. I could tell by the look on William's face he had never experienced anything like this before. Wendy, on the other hand, was ready to get loose. I don't know if she came from an Ivy League school or an uppity family. If she did, somewhere along the way, she was introduced to the wild side. She grabbed William by the hand, leading him to the dance floor as she bounced to the beat. Jackie and i followed alongside them. It was a sight to see Wendy getting loose. She wasn't the best-looking lady, but she was shapely, especially in the rear. She was working everything she had on him, which was too much for him to handle, as he tried to keep up to no avail. He was moving to the beat of a different drum. Jackie was all over him as the DJ spent another jam: "Ho's in the Club," by Tela. This was a song that I liked as well. It had a nice beat, the kind that makes you want to get some if you feeling real good. Jackie and I was doing the damn thang as she let her discreet freak come out in a ladylike manner. This DJ was good. He kept spinning hit after hit. The floor stayed full. The younger crowd was getting hype. Looking around, there were a lot of fine-ass ladies doing some dirty dancing, if you know what I mean.

We got our groove on for a little longer before taking seat out on the deck. As Jackie and Wendy removed their shoes to let their tired feet breathe, I noticed the happiness in them both. It was as if they hadn't had any real fun in a long time. While talking, Jackie drew in close to me, placing my hand in hers. I felt kind of warm inside.

I guess it has been a long time since I had any real fun too. I think it also had to with the fact it had been a long time since I felt about anyone the way I began to feel about Jackie. After the sex episodes we had, especially the one in the cabin, and seeing her tonight, who could blame a brother for feeling the way I felt?

It was now 2:45 a.m. Surprisingly, a lot of people were still out enjoying the calm ocean air. All partied out, we all decided to head to our cabins for the night.

The next day, in the afternoon, Jackie and I awoke to a beautiful Bahamian island. It was gorgeous—lovely palm trees, white sand beach, shapely women, clear blue water. The ship was docked for the remaining two nights of the cruise. It was time to explore the island. Jackie decided we'd begin the afternoon by going snorkeling. This always looked like it was fun from what I'd seen on television. It was a pretty thing to see the different species and colors of fish swimming in the crystal-clear water. The tour guide took us to a small body of water a few miles from the luxurious hotel/resort we were at. The location was great for swimming, with lots of swimmers and snorkelers all around us. Some of the people went into a cavern a few feet from where we were, but the guide said it was too dangerous for us to go. We finished up this adventure and were ready for another, so our guide took us to a land cave that was safe enough to explore. The cave was dark and damp and filled with bats. We went in one side through a long tunnel, which ended on the other side of the cave. As we were heading back to the ship, the guide informed us of the bonfire dance happening tonight, asking if we were going. We knew this was a big attraction for tourists, so we couldn't pass it up. We all said yes. According to the travel bureau, the bonfire would feature dinner cooked over a fire pit, music, native dance rituals, and a full bar—all on the beach. We'd enjoyed the events that took place so far but knew they were coming to an end, so we enjoyed the last night on the beach by making love. It was great feeling, the waves crashing onto the shore and upon us. I have to admit, this was a great getaway. I really enjoyed it, and I told Jackie. Not surprisingly, she responded the same way.

5

IT'S been two weeks since I kicked it with the fellas, which means I had to come up with a story for where I been. I also would have to make up for the slack I left to prove to Silencer I was serious about moving up in the clique. It was a cold night. Wasn't nobody out but a few lookout boys and a few runners. The runners was the customers from smokehouses coming to get the crack. I got to the spot ready to get busy serving packs. While walking up the stairs, I came up with an excuse for my disappearance: my mother was in the hospital dying from cancer. I got up to the door hoping they would believe me. If not, my whole operation would be jeopardized. Three knocks, I was in.

"What up! Missing in action" came from Red.

"Shit, just came back from down south, putting my momma to rest," I told him.

"Word. What happened?" asked Do-Dirt and Scooby.

"She had cancer."

"I'm sorry to hear that. That shit be taking a lot of people. That's how my grandmother died, dog," Silencer said as he dapped me and told me I was up.

That was easy. I thought it would be much harder. I hope it's over at that. You never know what Silencer really be thinking, he so quiet. I took my coat off, got comfortable, and waited for the customers to come.

Do-Dirt and Red were doing the usual, playing Madden, so I took the opportunity to get more acquainted with Scooby and Silencer. I started telling them about how my mother was fine and how she suddenly just started to shut down. I said I was holding her hand all while she was on the breathing machine in the hospital. Silencer asked me if she was suffering, because he remember when his grandmother had cancer, she was in a lot of pain before she died. I was glad to see he had a soft side and we had something to connect on (thanks to the bureau), so I kept on going. I told him that she wasn't at first. I remember her working up until her doctor appointments became so frequent, she had to stop working. But anyway, I was like, yeah she suffered in the end. She couldn't talk or breathe. I was holding her hand all the way through her last days. She looked me in the eyes before leaving. It might be sad to say, but I'm glad she ain't got to suffer no more. Hope she up in heaven looking down on me, talking God into forgiving me for what I'm doing.

Silencer nodded his head in agreement. I could tell he was feeling hurt by the way he got more relaxed and how the tone in his voice became calm and almost silent. Silencer was the leader of this crew because he was smart. He knew the game and could get into people's heads. The people he was leading, not including myself, didn't have any book sense or much common sense, which made it easy for him to manipulate them into doing as he commanded. This is the way of the pecking order on the streets. You start at the bottom and put in the work until you get rank, getting your own crew. If only the hustlers and gangsters would put more into doing something positive, they could get along in corporate America.

By now, we was just chilling, smoking one of Do-Dirt's tightly rolled blunts. The customers was coming but only in spurts. One minute it would be slow. Then it would be like twenty customers in one whop. The weather was freezing outside had something to do with it. But anyway, the work was moving. I went through $3,000 in a four-hour period. I thought we would be through for the night. Then Silencer brought out another stash of work he had bagged up. Still smoking, Silencer took the controller for his shot in Madden after Red's loss. I never got into video games, even as a kid, so I wasn't too anxious to play. I wouldn't play even if I wanted to. I had to put in as much work as possible to move up. Things were looking on the up and up. If Silencer was playing the game, he trusted that I could handle the customers who came short or with merchandise. His rule was don't take any shorts. No change. No sob stories. Nothing other than cash. I did the work like a true soldier—quick, tough, and thorough—sure to make Silencer notice.

Do-Dirt was a good worker but too immature to be a leader or anything other than a foot soldier—good to put in work. Scooby was too soft to move up. He wasn't even a good soldier, just kept around cause he and Silencer was schoolmates. Red, on the other hand, was a true contender. He was already Silencer's best worker. He was the enforcer. He punished Scooby, Do-Dirt, and the customers when they fucked up or got out of line. If I were to move up and not cause any drama in the clique, I had to get in real good with Red as well as Silencer so Red didn't feel like he was being shortchanged. If there was any tension between us, he might not have my back if needed.

I finished off my work the next morning. By ten, I was done ready to go get some sleep. Everyone else had fallen asleep around five. Before leaving I count checked with Silencer. He was the only one up. Not surprisingly, I never seen him get more than six hours of sleep since I was initiated into the crew. I told him I would be back later.

I went to my apartment to get some much-needed sleep and to update my file with the progress of the case. I kept the file in a covered hole in the closet wall so no one could find them. After updating the information, I took a shower before crashing on the couch. I slept for a few hours, waking up feeling refreshed. I made something to eat from the few groceries I had in the refrigerator: a hamburger, fries, and a glass of cherry Kool-Aid. While eating, I called Jackie. It had been two days since I seen her, hoping she would talk and not be mad because I didn't come home. I got her on the phone. I could tell she was mad by the way she answered. Guess she does have a limit to her tolerance. She immediately cussed me out, saying, "Where the fuck you at, and where you been?" I responded I was at my friend's house last night because I got too drunk to come home, and the other night, I was trying to see if I really wanted to take this relationship to the next level. She said, "Well, do you? I said yes. Her comeback was "Well, get your ass here and fuck the shit out of me."

I had to do it good so she could forget about the whole situation or I'd hear her fuss or mess up the bond we have. I also would have to tell her I had started hustling to prevent any future arguments over why I didn't come home. I'll tell her I don't keep any of the stuff or money in the house and I have my old apartment as a stash house. To pull this shit off, I think I'm going to have to do some serious vagina eating. Let me throw on a new set of clothes so I can get out of here.

During the unusually long drive over to her house, I was thinking about what I was into. I had moved in with the crew fast. I got into a serious relationship with a woman that I love just as much as I do Marcy—not supposed to happen—and I haven't talked to Marcy or the kids in two months. It always works better for undercover agents to bury their real life just as deep as their cover so they don't expose any weakness—rule number one from training.

I stopped off at the flower shop on my way to Jackie's house to get some roses to make my apology more sincere. I picked a dozen—eleven red roses with a single white rose in the center. This was a great combination. I hope she likes them. I got to the house and pulled into the driveway parking in the back of her car. I took the set of keys out of my glove compartment, got the roses, and headed for the door. I opened the door and there was Jackie, waiting with nothing on, looking stunning as usual. She took the roses from my hand as I closed the door. She expressed her liking for the roses, then threw them on the couch before ripping my shirt off. I was kissing her passionately while taking my pants and underwear off to get ready for another crazy-mad fuck session. We did oral, penetration, oral again, and penetration again before we was out for the count.

We woke at the same time before she had to go to work. While we were dressing, she stunned me when she said, "I know you hustling, Thomas." I was shocked. For the first time, she called me by my real undercover name, and she found out the truth without me telling her. I asked her how she knew. She said she got her ways and she just knew. Before she left, she just told me not to bring any in her house and to be careful, and she left it at that. If I didn't know Jackie, I would have never imagined she was as laid back and the freak she was. Her demeanor is calm, her look professional. Plus, she a religious type. I guess you could say that's a lethal combination, which makes up for the freakiness.

I left shortly after she did to head to the spot but was rerouted when I got a call from Silencer saying he wanted to meet me at my crib for a talk. I agreed to meet him there, but I am nervous as hell, because I don't know what's up. All kind of crazy shit is racing through my mind. I don't know if he found out my true identity and is coming to take me out, if he has someone holding the kids and Marcy, if he got Jackie, or what. I am just nervous.

I came to grips before I pulled up to the apartment. He was already waiting in front of the building. I quickly scanned the apartment in my head, making sure nothing was out of place, just in case I had to do some explaining when we got up there. The apartment was fine—nothing pertaining to the case or about my personal life was out for him to see, so we was cool. He made himself at home, as if he had come over a thousand times, which I didn't mind, but damn, he could have at least asked if he could go in my refrigerator before getting something to drink out of it. He got his bottle of water, then took a seat on the sofa, sifting through the *Jet* magazines I had laid out on the table. He began telling me how the apartment was nice and conveniently located for a spot. I was glad he started talking about that instead of what it could have been. It took a load off my shoulders. I agreed with him, saying, "Yeah, but the landlord would never go for that. She would put me out or call the cops."

He said, "She don't have to know with the type of spot I'm talking about, dog."

If he is getting at what I think he is, I'm happy as hell, because shit is moving in the right direction. I asked him if he was talking about turning it into a customer spot. He told me no, a weight spot.

I said, "But I don't move weight for you. Who going be running it?"

He replied, "That's what I came over here to talk to you about. You been doing real good at working the spot and all. I think you might do good moving up in rank. I been paying attention to your swagger and business skills. You a real soldier. I'm going to have you and Red working together, moving shit, you know what I mean?"

I was glad as hell. I said, "Cool, that'll work for me. When this going to happen?"

He said, "It already did. I got two keys in the trunk. I'm going to bring them up, show you how to weigh them and package them."

When he went down to get them, I quickly made a call to headquarters to let my boss know I was officially in. I didn't talk long because I didn't want to get caught. I was peeping out the window the whole time, watching so I could see when he was coming back in the building. I watched him pull a brown dufflebag out of what looked like a secret compartment from the trunk of a two-door Ford Tempo, which I had never seen until this day. I guess this was the car used to transport the heavy stuff, because it was inconspicuous, so the buys were less likely to pull it over. He came back in the building with the bag in hand. Before hanging up, I quickly gave a description of the car, along with the license plate number so we could get a trace on who the car was registered to and possibly get a wiretap in the car. He came in, then put the bag on the table, saying, "You ready for the big league, nigga?"

I responded, "Hell, yeah. I got your back."

He pulled out two kilos of coke and a scale. I asked him where the clientele was going to come from. He told me he had already taken care of that. I was to use a cell phone he gave me so only his customers would have the number. He told me to answer it, prepare the order, and serve them when they came. I was cool. It sounded a little risky, but I was down. I was glad to be at this stage, moving up. Would only be a matter of time before I became Silencer's right-hand man. Once we become tight, I would ride with him soon enough, meeting his boss and ending this case. I rolled up a blunt while he was weighing and bagging up the coke so we could start business. I smoked half the blunt before passing it to Silencer after he asked, "You going to share, nigga?"

I said, "My fault. I was in a zone."

He replied, "Cool. That's some good as shit, huh. Got it from them Jamaicans."

He told me to call Red to tell him to come on over so we could get started. While waiting for Red to come, Silencer and I had a talk. He was telling me how he trust me—that's why he moving me up—but just don't fuck him or it would be hell to pay. He also began telling me that if I did good with this shit, who knows where it lead, but no matter what, never let none of this shit go to my head. And the most important thing of all: never use this shit. Silencer was smart. He knew what using this could do by seeing what it did to customers. Being stuck on this shit is hell. The third rule he gave me was never let the bitches you fuck with interfere with you taking care of business. If possible, don't let them know shit about what you do, and don't let vagina get you stuck.

By this time, Red was calling on the phone to tell us to open the door. He got lost in the building. He found his way from the fourth floor into the apartment. Silencer had finished his part and given us our instructions before he collected the keys from Red. Red had driven the truck over, so Silencer could leave the Tempo with us. Before he left, he told us get tight, be cool, and have each other's back because we was going to be working together from now on while Scooby and Do-Dirt going to be working the other spot. He left us with the work and an ounce of weed.

ONE month into me and Red getting acquainted in our hustle spot, we were moving the weight at great speed. We became close buddies, but I still had my guard up, as I wanted to get closer to Silencer. Now that we wasn't at the bottom spot—street-level dealing—we had more time to go places hanging outside the spot. We frequented the mall, catching movies and riding around.

I was finding out a lot of things about Red by him being a big talker. I was glad Silencer paired us up, because I could use Red as an information tool to get in closer to Silencer. Some days, I would just sit back and listen to Red talk, finding out he was really into vagina, clothes, and weed. One day, we were talking, and I asked him how long he was hustling and why he started. I wasn't surprised by his answer. His father was involved with hustling, and his mother was a drug user by way of his father, so he had nobody to turn to for money and food.

As we were talking, I was thinking of a story I could use for my excuse for hustling, which was not going to be hard, because I had already told them when I was buying weed that I had lost my job. Good enough for me. I knew Red was a good hustler, but when it came to putting two and two together, he wasn't really book smart. I told him I felt his pain when he was done telling me his story. I was telling him I had no father at all, because my father had left my mother and me when I was six years old to be with another woman. I remember him coming over one time after that to bring me a Christmas gift, and I never seen him again.

This conversation exposed us to each other. Only mine was made up. His was true. I felt bad for him but knew he was still involved with doing bad things that he didn't have to. We ended the conversation at that to play a game of Madden. I wasn't never into playing video games, so I wasn't any good at them. To make it look like I knew how to play, I skimmed through the book to find out how to pass and run so it would look like I knew what I was I was doing. I picked the Dolphins as my team. Red chose the Packers. He was always animated when playing the game. It was like he got a chance to be a kid that he never was. The game started. He won the toss, so he got the ball first. He was excited, telling me to get ready for an ass whippin'. I played into the hype, saying, "You talk a good talk, but I don't think so." I got my ass kicked 56 to 7. The only reason I got 7 was because I got a lucky interception at my 12-yard line.

Things were going good for us, so good we moved through the first two keys (kilos of cocaine) in three days. We also went through five more with just Silencer's people and two with our new people. With things going good for us, things weren't so good at the other spot. It got raided by the police early one Sunday morning. They had this raid well planned, which is the only way they could have pulled it off from the details given by Silencer, Do-Dirt, and Scooby, all of whom were in. At the raid, they came in plain clothes, disguised as customers. They knocked on the door, faking like they had guns for sale, which anybody in the drug game was always willing to buy. After they got in, they all pulled out their guns, ordering everybody on the floor. After they secured the apartment, they radioed for the other officers to come up. Two other spots got raided that same evening. The other two were weed spots. Silencer called us to bail them out at a little after eleven the morning after the raid. It was surprising no one was kept guess they were waiting to catch us with something bigger, even though they caught them with four ounces of bagged-up rocks.

Now with everybody at my crib, we was officially a crew. All about hustling. The crew was to abide by the rules set forth by the leader. Silencer set the rules, asking for little input from us. Rule one: always respect each other. Rule two: never discuss crew business with outsiders. Rule three: never steal off the top. Rule four: never cut side deals with other dealers. Rule five: never snitch. Silencer made it loud and clear—you follow these rules, you move up, but you break any of them, you pay with your life.

Things were going smooth. We were moving our product like there was no tomorrow. With Scooby now in jail for eighteen months after taking the fall in the raid, we had to keep hustling to take our mind off his absence. Although I hadn't known him as long as the others, I still felt bad for him. He is a nice dude. I couldn't show how I really felt, which was that all of them should have been behind bars. If it were up to me, they would have been. I would lock them all up in the hardest prison. But hell, I forgot, that's why I'm working the case—to make that happen. I am Incognito.

Silencer got a call from someone on his cell phone in the middle of the night. Must be someone important, because he left in a hurry. I asked Red if he knew who Silencer was talking to. He told me not to worry about it. He get that call once a month. I was anxious to know, so I started thinking of a way I could squeeze it out of Silencer. Maybe it was his connect, Darius Brown, who I have to take down, or maybe it was someone higher. I'll find out soon enough. I made the best of not knowing, taking in some Indo smoke with the fellas. We didn't have the Playstation, which was taken from the other spot, which we found out by going back the day after they got out of jail. It was late, and I was tired, so I left Do-Dirt and Red be in the living room to go sleep in the bed.

I fell asleep not long after hitting the mattress. I guess staying up more hours than getting sleep let fatigue take over my body. I woke the next morning feeling refreshed, new, like I never felt before. I don't know why. I guess it was because the good sleep or the dream I had about Jackie. I had a dream that we got married and went on a honeymoon to Hawaii. I dreamed we were there for two weeks of fun. On our vacation, we had sex and more sex, even having threesomes with various nicely shaped Hawaiian women. One of the threesomes, I just watched as Jackie and the lady ate each other out, then took a two-sided dildo into their pussies. I watched in amazement, jagging off, coming in minutes, just after they did.

I might have been energized because I knew I would see Jackie today. I would somehow have to find a way to break away from them to get over there, since I had not seen her for a week. I would eventually have to bring her into the picture if I was going to continue seeing her so they wouldn't become suspicious that I always left alone. I guess I'll come out upfront and say I have to go see a lady I met before we hooked up.

7

N O W that I made it further up in the crew, I thought it was time to go brief the bureau on the advancements I had made (as if they didn't already know). I'll ask Jackie to go with me so we can make up for the week that I haven't seen or talked to her. When I get there, I can also see the kids and Marcy, whom I haven't seen or talked to for over four months. I'm sure Marcy will have a lot to say to me if she hasn't filed for a divorce. I wouldn't blame her. I have been gone for a long time without contacting her before, but I don't recall it being this long. I couldn't imagine what the kids are going through. I hurt even thinking about it. I'll worry about it later. For now, I have to get Jackie straight.

I knew she would be at work when I got there, the perfect time to prepare a meal to take her mind off the situation. I have always been a great cook, since I started cooking at age ten. I fried some chicken, made some rice, steamed some fresh broccoli, and baked a sweet potato pie to have for dessert. To really set the mood, I turned the lights down, lit some candles, then put on a classic soul CD. I was sure to make her forget about the situation after all of this.

I heard the door open while I was in the bathroom freshening up. I suddenly became nervous. I wasn't sure how she would react to me not calling or coming, but she did say she knew I was hustling. I heard the sound of her heels tapping on the hardwood floor, getting closer and closer, making me even more nervous. I put on my game face and couraged up as she stood in the frame of the door, looking fine as hell and vindictive at the same time. Once again, she surprised me. Here I am, thinking she was going to slap me, cuss me out, or do something, but instead she, just kicked off her shoes, wrapped her arms around my neck, and kissed me. I don't know why, but it appears nothing I do makes her angry—at least nothing I have done so far. I wonder if there is anything I can do to make her mad. I know if this had been Marcy, I would be in hell right now, and she is my wife, who I work to take care of.

Jackie said in a childlike voice, "You made us dinner boo. You didn't have to do that."

We then made our way to the kitchen. She began asking me what I been doing while I was away. Before I began to answer her, I thought about rule number two: never discuss business with outsiders. This was playing in my head, but I wasn't going to shun her off. Besides, she wasn't a threat. I trust her. I told her I was making moves, just selling bigger stuff to other dealers. I told her that the customer spot got raided, but I wasn't there, because I had already been moved up.

She asked, "Did anybody go to jail?"

"Yeah, but they got out—except one, who had to go back because he was the one that had to take the charge."

She replied, "I'm glad you weren't there. I don't know what I would have done if you had to take a case."

I don't know what I would've done neither. If she only knew the case would have been prolonged once the judge received word of who I was from the bureau. There would have been one of our top lawyers appointed to the case, posing as a public defender just to keep my cover.

After talking about the situation for a while, I brought up going to California on a vacation to Disneyland. I asked her if she had any vacation hours left.

She said, "Sure. When you want to go?"

"Let's book the flight now."

Not finishing our dinner, we both darted to the computer in a race to see who would win, laughing all the way there. I let her win to make her feel good, but I put forth a good effort to throw her off. I booked the flight using my debit card, tied to my checking account. I had been stashing the money Silencer had been paying me. I had saved up a little over eight thousand dollars, almost enough to buy a half key, which would bring me closer to meeting the main connect to him. I got a package deal on the vacation from an online travel bureau. I got five round-trip tickets with two cars and two rooms at a four-star hotel for $3,250. I bought five tickets because I had to include the crew on this flight to keep them unsuspicious of my loyalty. Besides, it would get me in good. While booking, Jackie asked why I was buying so many tickets if it's just two of us. I told her I wanted to bring the fellas so they wouldn't think I'm a cop or nothing, being gone so long with no excuse for leaving. She agreed, but for the first time, I think she got mad at something I did.

"I hope they don't have to be tagging along with us when we go out. Anyway, I'll just sit by myself on the plane and act like I don't know you to help you play it off."

I said I was sorry, but they had to come, then thanked her for understanding. We went to bed, not having sex. Instead I just ate her vagina until she fell asleep.

I hope Silencer agrees to come. He might not want to because of the business. If he asks where I got the tickets from, I'll have to say I won them in a contest or something to put pressure on him to say yes. Since they have never been anywhere outside Milwaukee, I will have to paint a really pretty picture of the place to entice him.

I hooked Jackie up so good last night, she didn't even mention anything about me not seeing her for the week. She just said if it happens again, at least give her call. I told her I would take the time out to do just that. We both walked out together. Before getting in our car, we embraced to kiss. She placed her thick, voluptuous lips on mine and gently slid her tongue in my mouth to finish it off.

I got to the spot in quick speed, ready to tell them about the trip. I thought about what I would say on the way over, and I came up with a great idea. I would say we been working so hard, not really enjoying ourselves. It is time we did something to refocus. I said this would be a great way to regroup and come up with some new plans to tighten our game. I also convinced them we might be able to find a nice connect after mentioning how many beautiful women there are there. Silencer took the bait. We were on our way to sunny California. The weather was warming up with the new spring season. It was sure to be nice back home. I love California, especially in the spring and summer months. During this time of year, the sky is clear, the ladies are wearing near nothing, and the beaches are full of attractions—especially Venice.

Boarding time was at seven o'clock, which was not long after Jackie got off from work. She works until five, meaning she would have to hurry home and leave right out. She would have to drive herself there and sit alone to go along with the plan. I didn't want them to even know I knew her, since it might be used against me in the long run. Silencer, Do-Dirt, Red, and me rode in the truck to the airport. That way, he could park in the safety of the airport so no one could steal it or break in to steal the equipment. They were all excited about the whole trip and getting on an airplane. Silencer kept his composure as the gangster he was, but I could still tell he was nervous about getting on an airplane that was about to take him over thirty thousand feet off the ground. The rest of them was talking real loud, showing their nervousness and immaturity about never leaving the hood. I looked around to see if Jackie was there, as boarding time was fastly approaching, but I didn't see her. I was worried she was going to cancel out because we weren't going to be together, but then I thought, *No, she wouldn't do that—or would she?* I relaxed and began to talk to Silencer to take my mind off her. Just as the plane was boarding, she made it to the gate. I seen her at the back of the line as I took one last look back before I walked through the tunnel leading to the inside of the plane. I was glad she made it. Now I'll have a nice flight.

We sat next to each other in the same row, me having a window seat, Silencer next to me, Red, Do-Dirt, and Jackie. The other seats in the row were taken by this white family, appearing to be going on a family vacation. I was glad to see them, because I knew Do-Dirt and Red wouldn't be likely to harass her with unwanted advances.

The plane lifted off the ground as scheduled. It moved fast down the runway, then in the air we went. The boys grabbed the armrests tightly while laughing as if we were on a rollercoaster as the plane climbed in altitude. We reached sixty-two thousand feet, and the plane was now flying smoothly. Silencer and I was talking over some plans he had if he got out the game. I was surprised he opened up willingly. I didn't even bring the subject up. I listened to him tell me his dreams, ideas on different topics, and things he had seen in the game. He began by telling me how he would love to just be able to have his own legitimate business, where he could make a lot of money without having to work real hard for it something, like real estate. He even said he thought about going to school for it. He didn't graduate from high school, but he did have a GED. He opened up to, me telling me how he felt about the police, how some of them be real cool as long as you be cool with them. He even told me how he got caught with some product one time, and they let him go for the small price of $2,800, which was under his car seat. He said they were no different than the average working joe. They had a job to do, which they probably didn't like, but they had to feed the kids and put clothes on they back. He also told me some stories about the ones that were assholes, straight dicks. He told me about one instance when the police beat down a dude he knew, then planted some drugs on him to take him to jail. To go along with him, I told him I know what he mean but said they probably be that way because all the stuff they put up with from people they come in contact with. I took a chance with that, but I wanted to see where he stood. I was lucky. He agreed. He replied, "Yeah, some niggas be acting a fool for no reason, trying to make the police mad, but sometimes they take it out on everybody else they stop. That shit ain't right." I agreed. We left the conversation at that.

Now done with our chitchat, Silencer leaned forward to check on Do-Dirt and Red after seeing them nervous from the turbulence the plane was experiencing. He asked, "Y'all aight niggas? Y'all ain't scared is y'all?"

Red replied, "No, we ain't scared. Just worried about what the hell going on with this muthafucka dog!"

Silencer replied, "Quit crying. Ain't nothing going to happen to us. It's just some wind blowing."

I took this opportunity to take a look at Jackie to see if she was alright. She was.

The plane landed at LAX as scheduled. As we touched down, the pilot announced the temperature. It was a sunny eighty-two degrees. Stepping off the plane into the baggage-claim area, we all went outside to wait for our luggage. The fellas was amazed at the beautiful palm trees and warm air. I was more than happy too. There's something about the smell of the hot LA air, even with the smog. It just makes you happy. Silencer was amazed too. He didn't let it show much, but you could tell he was glad to be out of Milwaukee. I asked him, "You cool, dog? How you like the look?"

He replied, "Yeah, I'm straight. Just taking in the air, getting a feel for the place. We going to have a good time. You know, live it up while we here."

"Okay, I feel you. Let's go get our luggage."

We grabbed our luggage, then walked to our car-rental shuttle. The shuttle bus would pick us up from the airport to take us the rental car area. We rented our car from Avis Rent-A-Car, a black Chevy Tahoe.

Jackie had rented her car from Avis too—a Lincoln LS. She was on the shuttle with us, still playing it off as if we didn't know each other. She was good. If I didn't know any better, I would have thought she was an undercover agent. Now riding in the bus with us, Do-Dirt decided to flirt with her. Surprisingly none of this happened on the plane. He asked her if she was from LA. She replied, "No, I am from Milwaukee. Why?"

His comeback was "Because if you was, I was going to ask you to be our tour guide."

Now I'm in somewhat of a panic because I don't know how far

he will go or if he will curse her out from rejection, but she can take care of herself. I was right. She politely turned him down, saying, "Thanks for the offer, sweetie. If I was from here, I would love to show y'all around. I just know about Hollywood Boulevard, the Walk of Fame. That will be nice to check out the names of the stars on the sidewalk."

He left it at that, saying, "Thanks."

She looked at me with a grin, turning her head back out the window.

After getting our ride, we headed to the Valadon Hotel, where we would be staying. It was a nice small hotel located off the Sunset Strip close to the hills. The hotel had a rooftop swimming pool, a gym, a hot tub, and a rec room. I knew about the hotel because this was used by the bureau in a sting operation on another case. During the ride to the hotel, the fellas gazed at the cites. We seen the House of Blues, Mann's Chinese Theatre, even the Mega Virgin Record Store. They were more than happy to see all the California ladies dressed in bikinis and two-piece gym clothes—the usual for a hot, sunny day.

I knew they would like the hotel by the look on their faces when we arrived in front of it. At this point, I didn't think it would have mattered if we was in a shack. They was just happy to be outside the confines of Milwaukee. We checked into our rooms, Do-Dirt and Red in one, me and Silencer the other. We agreed to shower up, then hit the streets.

I took the opportunity to make a couple of important calls while Silencer was in the shower. First, I called Jackie to let her know how she pulled things off and to tell her our plans for seeing each other. Then I called the bureau to check in, to let them know that I was in town. Lastly, I called Marcy. This was hard, because I hadn't spoken to or seen her or the kids in months. It felt really good to hear her voice.

I instantly came back to reality, remembering my mission. First thing I said was I love you. I told her I couldn't talk long but told her to be at Pinks, our favorite place, in about two hours. I told her not to bring the kids. I didn't want to take a chance on them blowing my cover since I hadn't seen them so long. Even though we had trained them on how to handle the situation of me being an agent, it was still too risky. I hung up in the knick of time. Silencer had just turned off the shower. I grabbed my change of clothes and hygiene items to take in the bathroom with me to take my shower.

After we both got dressed, we checked on Do-Dirt and Red to see if they were ready to go. They were. To keep things on schedule, I had to slide in the suggestion of getting something to eat so I could meet Marcy in time. While we were driving in the car I said, "Let's go grab a couple of hot dogs with chili cheese fries." They were up to it. This is what I liked—everything going smoothly. We went to Pinks, the famous hotdog stand, which Marcy and I along with everybody else in LA liked so much. It was packed as usual, but we waited in line anyway. I glanced around, noticing Marcy standing in line a few spots ahead of us. I immediately rubbed two fingers down the side of my face, our way of saying "I love you" when we met while I was undercover. We didn't usually talk, but in this case, I had to. As she was leaving, we were still in line. I asked her if she knew where we could find a mall. She gave us the directions to Fox Hills Mall over in Culver City. I said thank you, walking away from her, as it was time for us to order. It felt really good talking to her in person. We ordered our food to go. We each got two all-beef hot dogs, a tray of chili cheese fries, and a glass of lemonade.

We walked around the block, eating our food before getting in the car. We wanted to keep it clean just in case something spilled. In that case, we would have to pay for any damages.

Pinks was not too far from Hollywood Boulevard. It was located off La Brea and Melrose, about thirteen blocks. We could have walked if we wanted to, but none of us did, so we drove. We hit the boulevard in about three minutes. As usual, it was packed with tourists. We rode down from La Brea and Hollywood to Vine before finding a space to park so we could get out and walk amongst the people. Walking from Vine Street up, you got to see all of what Hollywood Boulevard had to offer. The stretch of the

Walk of Fame ended at Vine to the east and La Brea to the west. We got a chance to see the different shops that were on the boulevard, the famous people's sidewalk star, but most of all, we got to see the different people panhandling for change. Some of these people had some real far-out stories for why they were out there. Some had run away from their hometowns to come to Hollywood at a shot of stardom. You had some that ran away from home because of abuse. Then some just had nowhere to go. We were amazed at all the people who were homeless, just hanging out, doing nothing, something you don't see every day in the hoods of Milwaukee. We let that go by and began enjoying ourselves by talking about the foreign tourists—mostly Asian—that were snapping pictures of the different attractions.

We had stopped at a local novelty shop. I guess Silencer wanted to get some souvenirs to take back to remember our time here. I took the opportunity to get away by going to the bathroom at a pizza shop across the street. I called Jackie and let her know where I was. She told me she already knew because she was there too. She had been following us since we left the hotel. She seen us at Pinks, followed us to the boulevard, and now she was coming in the pizza shop. For some reason, I was not surprised at her. She was a hell of a woman. I was convinced this is one woman you don't want to rub the wrong way. She told me to stay in the bathroom so she could show me the surprise she got for me. I stayed in talking on the phone until she walked up to the door. When she got to the door, she told me to open it and hung up the phone. She came in, locked the door, then kissed me wildly. I kissed her back passionately, lifting up her dress and grabbing her ass in my hands before bending her over the toilet to give it to her doggy-style. I had to hurry because they were waiting for me across the street. Didn't want to stir up suspicion. I slid my hard erection into her moist vagina, pounding harder with every thrust, sending a stream of cum into her body after a short but long three minutes. After the sexcapade, we cleaned up, kissed, and parted as if nothing had just happened. I was getting a call on my cell phone just as I was approaching the crew. I could tell it was them because Do-Dirt hung up as I got there. I played it off like I had to take a shit from all the chili cheese fries.

Now that I had showed the crew a nice time, made contact with Marcy, been with Jackie, I had just one more thing to do before the trip was over: I somehow had to contact the bureau. I wouldn't be able to get away to meet at the diner. The contact was set to take place, so I had to improvise. I had to have someone come to the hotel. I called the office pretending to call directory assistance to get driving directions to the mall, which I already knew. I got one of the lead investigators on the phone and gave my location, using the hotel as my starting point. After answering a few questions with simple yes and no answers, they got all the information they needed, so I hung up the phone.

8

THE trip was a success. We took our minds off what was happening and the stress of being in Milwaukee. The plane landed in Milwaukee International at 5:48 p.m. Sunday night. With all of us being exhausted from the trip, the long layover in Phoenix, and the flight itself, we all just wanted to go to sleep. Silencer told Do-Dirt and Red they could go home to get some rest so we could be fresh for the serious business we had to start taking care of. I never knew they shared an apartment off of Seventy-Sixth and Bremen, not too far from Erica's house. I found out where they lived when Silencer was leaving because he gave me the address with instructions to pick them up in the morning at ten sharp. Silencer had his own place, which I already knew—just didn't know where. I never pushed the issue, because Do-Dirt and Red didn't know where it was either. Just part of the game. The big man always kept a spot that the crew could kick it at but never let them kick it at the house he called home. I gave Silencer some dap, telling him glad he decided to take the trip and to be safe.

I was glad to finally be alone for some real rest. I took a shower and just chilled in my boxers. I waited for an hour to make sure none of them would be coming back before calling Jackie. I dialed her on her cell phone and got no answer. I then dialed the house. The phone rang four times before the answering machine came on.

For a moment, I was worried. I got ready to leave my message, then her soft voice answered, "Thomas. Hey, baby."

I answered back, "Hey, baby. You made it in safe huh."

Jackie replied, "Yeah, I'm safe. Just tired and lonely. Need to be held by your soft, strong hands. Think you up for the challenge?"

"Yeah. In fact, I was thinking about you too. Thinking how I want to rub up against the softness of your body, smell the sweet nectar of your honey juices, and hear the whispering softness of your voice."

She replied, "Is that right? Well, come on over."

I said I would, but tonight the apartment was mine to myself. "Why don't you come over here?" I said. "I know it's risky, but it's cool. They all going to they real homes and won't be back out, so it's cool. Besides, we can think of a way to introduce our relationship."

I gave her the address. She said, "I'll be there soon." Then the phone went dead.

Jackie got there in fifteen minutes flat. She arrived in nothing but a brown rain jacket. I was glad to see she didn't have anything on underneath. Means we were going to be doing the do all night, or at least half the night anyway.

I threw the jacket on the floor, then led her straight into the bedroom. She went right to my penis, taking it in her mouth. She gently caressed the head with her tongue between strokes. She did this so good she was like a monster vacuum cleaner, sucking in dirt. I came in her mouth real fast. She sucked up every last drop, swallowing it without spitting. I was now ready to return the favor. I immediately laid her back legs, spread tall in the air, then went in for dessert. I licked all around the lips, then focused on the clit. I licked it, sucked it, nibbled it, and then blew on it, sending her into a frenzy before sticking my tongue into her hole. I went in and out, stroking the walls, catching a gush of sweet creamy nut on my last stroke.

Both of us being fully satisfied with our orgasms, we just cuddled for a little while, talking about the trip. I told her she did an amazing job pretending we didn't know each other even when Do-Dirt asked where she was from. I for sure thought that would have led to further conversation. I then said, "While we on the subject, we're going to have to come up with a way to hook up so it don't look like we already know each other. Maybe if we meet at the mall or at the cell phone shop, that would be better. I could go pay my bill Saturday, and you could be there too. What you think?"

"That's cool. That way, I could come on to you and give you my phone number to call me so then we could be legit. I mean for real legit."

"Yeah. Damn, baby, how come you so cool?"

"I don't know. That's just how I am. Well, I have to get ready to go. You going to walk me down?"

"Yes, I am, gorgeous. Anything else you want me to do?"

"Just be at the Sprint store over on Seventy-Sixth and Capitol, tomorrow at 6:30."

"I got you, boo. I love you."

"I love you too."

The next morning, Silencer came over bright and early. Must have been around nine. I was just getting out of the shower when the doorbell started ringing. I let him up, then finished getting dressed. He was waiting on the couch while I did what I had to do still. He began telling me he thinking about moving me up to general, a top position in the organization. He said I demonstrated all the right skills and put in enough work already to have the title. I also had the respect of the other crewmembers. After asking me how I felt about the move, he said he just had to run it by the colonel before it could happen. I was happy he mentioned this, for it was my golden opportunity to see who it was. I asked him if I was going to meet him, thinking he was going to say yes, only to get "Slow down, easy rider. When the time is right, you'll meet him." I was anxious now, because I never seen anyone other than Silencer, Do-Dirt, Red, and Scooby. Made me think it ain't nobody else. I was even wondering if the investigation was a case for the local gang and narcotics unit, not the FBI. I hadn't heard mention of any other names, like Darius Brown, which I was keying in to get. We left it at that, then headed out to pick up Do-Dirt and Red.

Silencer called Red on his cell phone while driving over there, telling him to make sure they was ready; we was on our way over to get them. I guess he forgot he told me to pick them up last night. Guess he must have cancelled his plans. Well, I was driving, so I headed on over to their house, hopping on the freeway. I made it there in no time. The freeway is usually empty this time of morning the early morning—commuters already making it to work. They were waiting downstairs in front of what appeared to be a nice building, along with Tracy and Erica. Red and Do-Dirt approached the truck, leaving the girls behind on the steps. Giving dap and what-ups, Red asked if it would be okay for the girls to get a ride to they cribs. Silencer agreed, telling the girls to get in. when they were getting in, he said, "Y'all ain't no strangers. Show a nigga some love. Shit."

Erica said, "What up, Incognito, Silencer? What y'all been up to?"

We answered back in unison, "Just chillin."

We dropped Erica off first, then Tracy. Since we were already in the area, we hung out around the old spot for a while, talking to old customers. It was a nice day out, which made the people come out to enjoy. The projects and hood was always live, especially when the weather was hot. Being forced inside during the winter months, you only had one thing to do in the spring and summer months— act wild and burn off all the laziness. Silencer was being asked by the customers when he was going to open up shop again, because they missed us being around there. The customers said the other dealers didn't treat them like we did. Hearing this made him feel good. You could tell because he was grinning from ear to ear while playing with the fake leg of one of our old customers, Phil. Phil was a Vietnam vet who had lost half of his leg in the war. He was a funny old dude who Silencer liked playing with. They kind of had a father-and-son relationship. From what we discussed in our meeting before, I knew we wouldn't be opening up shop again because of the raid, making my place the official spot. Silencer said because the police been watching so long now, they caught something. They'll keep trying to they get a case on him, so he won't open another spot in Cornell. He did, however, supply some of the other street hustlers.

We chilled for a little while longer with Tracy, who now brought out Shelly and Tanisha. I didn't want to run into Shelly, because I thought she might be tripping about me not calling her again, but she was cool. I guess she realized it was just a sex thing. Shelly and Tanisha both spoke. Shelly said to me, "What up, slickster?" in a happy around-the-way-girl tone.

I replied, "Shit, just chilling."

Red, seeing that she was feeling me still, tried to hype things up by saying, "She sprung. That nigga put the P down on her."

Shelly responded, laughing, "Shut up, Red. I ain't sprung. The penis was good, but don't get it twisted. I can get more. Please believe."

I jumped in, "Y'all ass crazy." I didn't say nothing more because I didn't really want to be bothered with the situation. I was glad when Tanisha took the conversation over, telling us about stuff that was happening. She told us about the night before, when two customers was fighting in the parking lot over who was sleeping with who. It was this gay couple; one got caught in the car getting fucked by another man. She told us the dude broke all the windows out before the man drove off.

"Shit was always crazy around here," Silencer said.

We started to make our way back to the truck so we could smash out when Tanisha asked, "Where y'all at now?"

Silencer replied, "We got a spot over by Westvillage now. Just a lay-low place, not like this one was. Why? You want to come over?"

Tanisha said, "Yeah, come pick me up tonight."

Silencer told her to give him a call later for a pick-up time.

Later that night, we was chilling at the spot when Silencer got the call. It was a few minutes past nine when Tanisha hit him up. They talked shortly before he headed out the door. When he left out, he said, "I'll be back soon. Be ready. We might have a winner."

Do-Dirt and I were playing the game while Red was sitting on the couch, smoking up the whole blunt. I suffered another loss, as usual, so I handed the controller to Red in exchange for what was left of the blunt. Soon after their game started, the door opened. It was Silencer and Tanisha. We thought they would have brought someone else with them, but she was alone. Tanisha took a seat, then asked us to roll another blunt. Silencer took off his coat, then began rolling. We all was talking, just parlaying, halfway through our second blunt and listening to a Twister track, when Tanisha stood up and started feeling herself. The song "Get It Wet" kept playing, and she kept feeling, except now taking off clothes as well. After removing her shirt and bra with her nice firm breasts exposed, she said, "I want to fuck all of y'all."

We were all already shocked by her taking off her clothes, but even more so now by her revelation. We quickly came to when she asked if we was down. She gave us a stipulation, though. We could not tell Shelly and the other girls. We agreed, and she proceeded to take off her clothes. She had a nice body even with the few stretch marks that lined her stomach. Now all of us being high and aroused, ready to get some, Silencer asked if I had any rubbers, because he was going to go first. He had one he got from his truck. I had a box in the room I kept just in case I ever had company over, so Red, Do-Dirt, and me was cool on that tip too. Silencer led Tanisha to the bedroom so they could do their thing. We heard her moaning from in the living room, so Do-Dirt moved in to the door to hear, as he was getting more excited. The moans lasted for a short time longer before a sweaty Silencer exited the room. I was nervous now, scrambling my thoughts, because I didn't want to partake in this. This was degrading to her, but it wasn't rape. She did ask us to do it. However, I was still uncomfortable. Still thinking, I told Do-Dirt to go next. He came out as quick as he went in; it couldn't have been no more than four minutes. He came out half-naked, draped only in his boxers, saying she had asked for Red. I was glad, because I still wasn't ready to go in, so in went Red. Now, to play it off, I asked if it was good. They both replied it was good, wet, and warm—just right for a nut. I then asked if it was tight. Silencer answered, "Tight enough to feel the inside. You going to feel it."

Red was now coming out the room, smiling. It was my turn. I went in thinking she was going be tired just laying there, but she was dancing to the music still. She told me to come to her by pointing her finger at me and moving towards me. I went in. She softly stroked my penis until it became hard, then started sucking it. It was feeling good. I was almost ready to come, so I pulled back. She then turned around and put my penis in her vagina. I went in and out a few strokes before reaching a half-enjoyed orgasm. We dropped Tanisha off shortly after.

N O W with the crew knowing me and Jackie as a couple from us meeting at the cell phone store, things could start moving forward without me having to sneak away to call or see her. We met on Saturday, just as planned. I took Silencer, Red, and Do-Dirt with me to pay my bill so Jackie could meet me there we arrived at 5:45 p.m. We were waiting for my payment to go through when she walked in. She spoke to us as a group.

"How y'all doing tonight?" She went to get help from the store attendant. She looked over at Do-Dirt, then the rest of us, saying, "Didn't I see y'all on the plane?" After a moment of silence, everyone excitedly said, "Yeah, we sat next to you."

Do-Dirt said, "You still not ready to give me the number?"

Jackie replied, "No disrespect, but I was digging your friend over there. He seem more my speed. It ain't going cause no static between y'all if I give it to him, will it?"

Do-Dirt said, "No, it's all good. Do your thing, ma."

Now that I had my transaction complete, Jackie gave me the number on the way out the door, telling me to call her later. She then said a smooth goodbye to us, "Y'all be easy out there."

We decided to go get something to eat over at Tasty's, a fish and chicken shack, after leaving the phone shop. During the ride over, Do-Dirt told me to tear that vagina up for him when I hit it because she was hella fine. I wanted to tell him I already did and the shit was good, but I couldn't do that, because it would mess everything up. I'll just wait until she come over one night while their getting ready to leave. I told him, "Yeah, I plan to hit that shit soon. I'm going to call her to see what's up in a day or two make her want me more."

He said, "I feel you."

We ordered our food to go because we did not want to eat there. It was on the wrong side of town, and none of us were strapped.

Back at the spot, while eating, we discussed business. Silencer told us we were doing a great job getting money, but we needed to expand our business to other areas. He wanted to go into selling weed as well as cocaine. Silencer had made a connect with the Jamaicans with the potent weed that we would buy from at whole-sale price if we bought ten pounds or more (some new information for the bureau). Silencer appointed Do-Dirt and Red to sell the weed. With Scooby in jail, it was just Silencer and me. I was now his right-hand man. First thing in the morning, we was to meet with the Jamaicans to purchase twenty pounds of sticky light green weed, better known as skunk. The price we would pay: $7,500. We had already but ten keys of the cocaine we were selling, which we sold six of so far. It was time for Do-Dirt and Red to be the soldiers they are and come up. I had shown my skills, which is why I moved up so fast. I was now ready to step it up another notch so I could get to the main person and get this case over with. With our new branch of service, we now needed a new spot for Do-Dirt and Red somewhere close to the old spot but not in the same building. The look was on. Searching the classified ads and driving the neighbor-hood, we came across a building three blocks down and two blocks over from Cornell. We would have to find someone to get the apart-ment for us because the landlords usually never rent to young black males, especially in this neighborhood, and we didn't want the place in our name if the police raided. In this situation, we normally got some girl or customer to rent the place. Silencer paid Tanisha one hundred dollars to rent the house. This was a nice place. It was a single-family house with two bedrooms and two bathrooms. This was just right for a weed spot. There were only three other houses on the block and a big field. The other house was on the sides of this one being on the left across the alley, one to the right, and the other across the street on the corner. The rent was modestly priced at $450, which was nice. Not that we would have a problem paying more. We were moving heavy quantities of our products so money was not an issue.

Even though we had now incorporated Tanisha into our crew, we still kept her in the dark about what we were moving and what we discussed about the business amongst ourselves. She was the right element to have in the clique for several reasons. One, she was always willing to fuck us or give some good head when needed and we couldn't get elsewhere. Two, she was laid back but could get dirty if needed. Three, if we needed to get at some niggas, we could use her as bait to lure them motherfuckers into our reach. Last but not least, she was funny and just real cool to kick it with.

After getting the place, we had to go shopping for furniture to make it more homely. It wasn't too many rooms we had to fill, so it wasn't a problem getting a nice deal for five rooms of quality furniture. The Arab stores always had specials running. Three, four, five, even seven rooms for as little as $699. We ended up getting the furniture for the living room, dining room, and two bedrooms for $1,650. It was two queen-sized beds, two dressers, and two night-stands. The living room and dining room furniture was $400. That included a small table and four chairs for the dining room and a three-piece sectional for the living room. We didn't get any for the kitchen because there was a table, refrigerator, and stove already there, which was left behind from the previous occupants. Our final piece of furniture was a weight set for the basement.

Now we were in a new area. Even though it was on a total of seven blocks from the original spot, we had to lay back and scope the area out. We had to watch the block for other hustlers that might be there. We had to see if there were nosy block watch neighbors. We also had to watch to see if there were late-night creepers, the thieves.

This was going to be Do-Dirt's and Red's job, since they were going to be the ones primarily there. Silencer and I had my place as the spot we would be operating. It was a group of six dudes that always hung out in front of the laundromat on the corner. We wasn't sure if they were hustling, but they likely were, making them a possible problem if they felt we were moving in on they territory or if they felt we were balling—which we were—and they wanted to pull a jack move. We left Do-Dirt and Red with some straps and told them to be careful.

Now that Do-Dirt and Red were doing their own thing, it was time to get down to serious business for Silencer and me. We started hanging like two peas in a pod. It was like we became brothers overnight. Where he went, I went, and vice versa. I even started taking him over to Jackie's house with me, when she wasn't there mostly, to show him I trusted him and thought he was cool enough to bring him to her crib. I was shocked when one day, he took me to his mother's house. I had been to the house before, but not being able to go inside, I never knew who lived there. He took me in this Monday to meet her. When we got in front of the house, he said to me, "I want you to come in to meet my mother, so be cool on the language and loudness."

I replied, "Cool, dog. I got respect for that."

His mother was a heavyset older woman. She had a head full of grayish black hair, heavy bags under her eyes, and what appeared to be a limp from being on tired legs. It looked as if she had plenty of restless nights, probably from worrying about Silencer. She spoke to me in a country-like motherly voice, "Hi, baby. What yo name is?"

"Michael," I responded.

"That's a nice name. So you friends with Marcus?"

"Yes, ma'am."

"Good. He a nice boy. He can be stubborn sometime, but he a nice boy."

"Yes, he is. That's why I became friends with him."

She laughed, saying, "Y'all met in the projects over there?"

"Yes, ma'am, we did."

"I hope y'all ain't getting in no trouble over there. It's so dangerous in there."

"No, ma'am, we ain't getting in no trouble. We mostly be at my place. It ain't in the projects."

"That's real good." You seem like a nice young man. You stick with my baby all right."

"I will."

We left right after the conversation that we had, which Silencer didn't take part in because he was in the bathroom for the whole time. If I had to put money on it, I would bet that is where some of his money was kept. As we were leaving out the door, his mother gave him a kiss on the cheek and told us to be careful in them streets.

In the truck, I said, "So your name, Marcus huh?"

"Yeah, but don't be calling me that shit. I hate that name." I asked why. He said, "Because that's my father name. That punk motherfucker left me to be with a punk-ass dope fiend bitch who turned him out. Now he be buying that shit. He was buying from me at Cornell. Probably buying from somebody else in there."

I replied, "That's some fucked up shit, man. I feel your pain."

We left it at that.

We went to the spot to wait on some players in the game that was to buy two keys from us. They were some regulars, two young-ass niggas from on the west side of town. They always copped two keys every month, like clockwork. They got them for a good price, since they were loyal, coming across town to buy when they could easily buy from niggas in their hood. When they got there, a half-hour after we did, they came up with a black book bag on the back, like always—same routine. They came in counted out $62,000 in hundreds, fifties, and twenties, like always. We then gave them two bricks, uncut. As usual, Duwayne, the younger one of the two, sampled the shit by taking a line up the nose to make sure it was good. Before they left, Silencer asked them why they came all the way across town to us. They answered, "Because y'all got the potent shit. Them niggas on our side got that cut shit. We be booming y'all shit to our niggas so the fiends can only buy from us."

"Okay. We feel y'all. Keep it coming. Maybe we could get together and do bigger thangs. Peace."

We stayed at the spot for the rest of the afternoon and evening, making deals moving product. We got through the remaining kilo by breaking it down, serving three old-schoolers who had been in the game a lot longer than we had. They just never made it to the top. One of them was on a half-kilo, one on an eighth of a kilo, the other on two ounces.

After them, we closed shop for the day to head home. Silencer went to his crib. I went to Jackie's. I stopped off in Cornell before heading to Jackie's to see if Shelly was around. I don't know why I hadn't talked to her since our last rendezvous. I wasn't even sure she would talk to me, but I wanted some super head (blowjob), so it was worth a shot. I made it over there in little time parking in the parking lot seeing all kinds of people out. I was still in the Honda, which I desperately needed to trade in now I got a little money, but later for that. I called Shelly on the phone only to find it disconnected, which means I would have to go to her apartment. Walking to her building, I was being hit up by all the customers out there.

"You got some work, Incognito? You got something?"

I had to turn them all away because I didn't have any. I told them all the same thing we told them before, "We ain't got no shop here no more," and I continued on my way. I knocked on Shelly's door three times real hard, trying to sound like the police to see if I could scare her, if she was even there. After I knocked again even louder, she answered, "Who the fuck is it?"

I yelled, "It's the police. We got a search warrant. Open the fucking door."

She opened the door, saying, "Your ass crazy. Don't be doing that shit. You almost scared me. But what's up. I ain't seen or heard from you in a minute."

"I know, I been busy. I was just coming by to see how you was doing."

She came back with, "Don't play me. Your ass want some pussy, don't you?"

"No, I just want to talk to you."

"Come on in."

"No. Come out to the car."

"Well, come in while I put some shoes on and throw my hair into a ponytail."

"Okay, that's cool."

I was waiting on the couch for her, and out the back comes these two little boys. I didn't know if they were hers or not, because the conversation never came up the couple of times we kicked it. These was some be-be kids too. I mean, they was asking me all kinds of questions and climbing all on my legs and lap. I had to fight them off practically. It took her ten minutes to get ready. I guess she was in the bathroom taking a ho bath (using a towel to wash her vagina and ass) and brushing her teeth, because I heard the water running and some gargling. She came out looking nice for the quick trans-formation. She yelled at the kids to go in the back with whoever was back there. We walked to my car, sitting in the car with my tinted windows. I drove to a secluded parking lot in the complex. We began talking for a while before I asked her to suck my dick. At first she looked at me crazy but gave in with a little persuasion. I told her that I would come over again tomorrow to take her to the movies and out to dinner. I knew I was lying, but I still wanted to get a blowjob from her because she did it so well. She took it in her hands to get it up a little, then put in her mouth. I just lay back in the seat waiting to get off, which didn't take long. After accomplishing my mission, I went on to Jackie's.

When I got to Jackie's, she was asleep. I woke her up because I hadn't seen her in two days and needed her to talk to me, since I didn't have Marcy to hold or talk to. We started to talk about how our day went. She told me her day was fine. She didn't work hard at all. She told me she got a bonus for getting a big-ticket client for the company. I congratulated her on the accomplishment, then gave her a kiss. She told me she went to her mother's house to take her out to dinner to celebrate. I asked how was her mother, since I hadn't seen her for a while (about a month). I was told everything was going fine with her, and she asked about me. She wanted to know how I was doing.

Jackie put on some soft music and opened a bottle of white Zinfandel wine to set the mood for our romantic night. I could tell she was horny from the negligee she was wearing. It was a pink two-piece with the front cut out of the panties. I was happy to see her in it, because, as usual, I was more than happy to fuck her freaky ass. We didn't get to the sex right away, just talked and listened to the music until the wine kicked in for her and the moment was right. When she felt it, she started kissing me on my neck and nibbling my ears. The way she did that made me weak. It was very passionate and soft. I reciprocated everything she did to make her hot and wet so I could have her ready for me to penetrate her with my now hard penis. The clothes came off, and the fucking began. We sixty-nined first, then I hit it missionary style (legs together up in the air). I turned her to give it to her in her favorite position, doggy style. I wasn't ready to climax since I'd already had one orgasm tonight with Shelly. I usually climaxed pretty fast, but after the first one, I was pretty much ready for the battle. I had a problem with Marcy because she always complained I came too fast. I don't know if it was because I was with her long enough not to care if she got hers or if it was just too good, but with Jackie, I wanted to last, because I wanted to satisfy her. On this night, I did it pretty quick. I pounded the hell out of her from the back, then laid her on her back halfway off the bed and lifted her in the air from the waist so her back could be arched. That way, I could hit her G-spot, which made her moan louder and reach her peak faster. I had learned how to do that by watching *Talking Sex* with Ruth Johnson, a late-night sex show where callers called in to get advice on sex from an old white lady. When she came, she exhaled a few deep breaths and thanked me for the good sex.

The next day, I got up early to make us breakfast so we could start our day off good and energized. I made pancakes, bacon, eggs, and grits. It was smoking good too. I poured glasses of orange juice for us, then went to get her up so she could come eat. She went to the bathroom to freshen up before coming to eat. We ate while talking and watching *The View*. We had good chemistry together at the table that morning. I thought about what my life might have been like had I met her in college and married her instead of Marcy. I pictured us having a good time walking on the beach, going to work every morning, and coming home at the same time, smiling to see each other. I wasn't an agent in this fantasy; instead, I was a district attorney (something I often thought about being in real life). The thoughts faded as we finished our food. It was time for her to get ready for work, so we jumped in the shower together. I washed her back. Then she washed mine. We jumped out after a quick five minutes.

Jackie looked stunning when she got dressed. She had put on a black two-piece suit with a burgundy blouse under the vest. She had it buttoned up just enough to show the crevice of her firm, round breasts. Her hair and makeup were flawless. The mascara had her eyelashes full and long. The foundation gently highlighted her dimples, and the red lipstick enhanced her set of full lips. She was remarkable. I asked her if anything important was going on today. She told me she had a power meeting with the CEO of the big corporation she landed. I told her from the way she looked, I wouldn't be surprised if he asked her out or offered her a better position at his firm. I gave her a kiss before she headed out the door, and she asked me from her car was she going to see me tonight. I told her I don't know, it depended on what goes down today. She got in the car and drove off.

I got dressed after putting another $3,000 with the $27,000 hidden in one of my suitcases in the closet I was given. It was hot out today, so I threw on a pair of black gangster Levis with a gray wife-beater (tank top), a pair of black and white Air Maxes, and a black LA Dodgers hat. I was fresh to death.

I called Silencer to see where he was at before leaving so I could see what kind of time I had before I went to the spot. He told me he was going to his mother's house to drop something off (my guess, another cash drop). Then he would meet me at the spot. I said, cool, see you later. I left so I could have enough time to stop at the record store. I wanted to get a new CD, some real gangster shit to keep me in character. I had to listen to all the shit that came out to keep me on my game. I had learned a lot of the street smarts I knew from listening to the rap music bought at the bureau and some of the criminals I arrested while I was a street cop. I immediately put the CD in, blasting the volume as I had a booming system. The song that played was "Meal Ticket." This was almost every gangster's theme song for a while, just as every other No Limit CD put out. I let the CD play and just rode.

The spot was about ten minutes away from the record store, which was located on Martin Luther King Drive (a street in the ghetto of every major city). I made it there in seven minutes. Silencer was still not there waiting in front, like I thought he would be. By the way, today we going to get the nigga a key to the apartment. I was glad he was not there because it gave me time to update the file of information I had on him. I took the file out of the secret hiding place, quickly updated what had transpired with the case, and then locked it back up. I didn't know what was taking him so long, but I wanted him to hurry up, because today was the day we had to re-up (get more product) since we had sold out the night before. We would also have to check up on Dirt and Red. I called Silencer on his cell phone to see where he was at. When I heard a knock at the door, it was him. He told me he got in when some fine-ass lady was going out. I asked him if we were going to get back on today. Already two people called asking when. He answered, "Yeah." he made a call and started talking I was hoping to hear a name but no luck. The conversation was short and brief. He said, "Five and two," then hung up the phone."

I wanted to know what that meant, so I asked, "What that was about?"

He answered, "Five of them thangs in two hours. Don't worry. You'll know all my terminology soon enough."

I said, "Cool."

We had to go over to the weed spot to see what they had left before going to meet the cocaine connect.

We pulled up on the block and seen the same group of niggas hanging in front the laundromat. The laundromat was connected to a store, so we stopped to get some Phillies so we could roll up some stuffies when we got to the spot. Silencer parked the truck and put the 40 Glock he kept, which was always in a secret compartment his grandfather installed for him, in his waist under his shirt. He said, "Let's go together in case we have some trouble from these fools."

We got out together and walked up to the door. They didn't say nothing, just looked at us crazy. When we got in the store, we noticed Dirt in there getting some Phillies. Look like they had the same idea as us. When we left the store, as we were getting in the truck, one of the dudes hit Dirt with a cork from a champagne bottle. He didn't say sorry or anything, just gave a cold look.

Dirt said, "Man, ain't you going to say excuse me or something?"

The dude said, "For what?"

Dirt said, "You just hit me with that muthfuckin' cork."

The dude then said, "That's some tough shit. What you going to do?"

As all of them were approaching, Silencer pulled out the Glock and pointed it at them. They stopped in their tracks. Silencer said, "It ain't going to be no jumping. Let them go head up."

The leader of their crew said, "That's cool. Whip that nigga, Bones."

Bones was a tall, slinky dude with cornrows. He stepped to Dirt trying to hit him, but Dirt avoided his hit. The dude grabbed Dirt. That's when Dirt started to push in Bones's eye with his thumb. Bones let him go, and Dirt grabbed him threw him to the ground. While he was on the ground, Dirt started stomping him. He stomped him so bad, Silencer had to grab him off. After Bones got up, the leader reached out his hand, balled in a fist, saying, "Y'all cool."

Silencer, with Glock still in hand, dapped fists with the dude and backed away to the driver side of the truck. We talked about the shit, congratulating Dirt on whipping that nigga. Silencer said, "I don't think we going to have no problems out of them niggas, but be careful, just in case. When y'all want something from that store, walk together and stay strapped." Dirt agreed to the demand.

Inside now, we rolled up two stuffies. The rotation started with Dirt, since he had just did a celebratory thing, followed by Red. Silencer asked how much weed they had left and was told an ounce. He counted the money they had, then put enough in his pockets to score with the Jamaicans again, leaving the rest on the table, telling dirt to find a hiding place in the house. We finished the blunts, then headed out. It was only twenty minutes left before we had to meet the connect. Normally, I would have been nervous, but the weed had me calm. We pulled up in back of a house, sitting in the alley away from the other houses that was in front, close to the sidewalk. I waited patiently while he was in there, and it did take quite some time. Some forty-five minutes later, he came back to the car. We always drove when transporting product, with five kilos in a black duffle bag. He apologized to me for taking so long before telling me they had to count the money. We got the keys at a great price, $24,500 apiece. On our way to the storehouse (spot), Silencer said, "After we serve a couple of people, we're going to head to the car lot. Time for us to get some new rides. Especially you, dog!"

I was happy ass hell. I got tired of riding the piece of shit I had.

We went to the car lot driving all three vehicles—the truck, my car, and the transport car—so we could trade them in. Silencer knew the salesman from buying the truck. We purchased a '98 Buick Regal, a '91 Chevy Camaro, and a '95 Chevy Blazer for $25,000 after we got $7,000 off the trade-ins. Silencer had the Blazer. He liked trucks. I got the Camaro because I had one in Belleview, and the Regal was for the transporting.

To celebrate, we went directly to the rims and stereo shop to get some rims for the Blazer and hook up the stereo system that came from the Suburban. We didn't get any on the Buick, but I did get a pair of chrome Daytons and a small stereo system. While the cars were being serviced, we went to the spots to break down the work and package it up. We took the weed to the spot before going to pick up the cars. The dudes that we got into it with were out on the corner, as usual. They must have smelled the weed smoke from the blunts we were smoking because they came walking down the street towards the car. By the time we had got on the porch, they had made it to the house. The leader, whose name was Solo, had called Silencer to the side to talk. Still wary of the situation that had previously occurred, Dirt and Red went into the house to grab the straps we kept on hand. The straps of choice were always Glock. We had 9 millimeters for the spots, each with a sixteen-round clip. I stayed out with Silencer just in case something jumped off, not that he couldn't handle it, because he had his 40 Glock. When they parted, we went into the house to get an ounce of weed for them. He told them the price is normally $125, but this one was on the house, as long as they came back to purchase more. They agreed. Silencer told us the reason he gave it to them was because he had intentions of making them our ally, not our enemies.

10

SILENCER gave me four customers to serve on my own because he had bigger customers to serve. The customers he now served bought half-keys or whole ones. The customers he gave me were buying eights or smaller pieces. I started to venture off on my own occasionally to find more customers. When I wasn't with Silencer or chillin with Dirt and Red, I was at Jackie's or hangin at the lake to seek out more customers. I caught three customers one day that wanted a connect on a half-key. I was glad to take them on because that meant Silencer had to buy more weight, so it wouldn't be long before he started to get questionedabout how he was moving the shit so fast. I ran the new customers by Silencer to see if he wanted to meet them. He told me when the time was right, he would but not now, just in case they wasn't legit (in other words, if they was the law).

I was doing well for two months, making enough to buy three keys of my own, including the money I had saved. Silencer congratulated me on doing so well by throwing a party for us at Matt's. Yep, the very club where Mr. Darius Brown was king. I knew it wouldn't be long before I crossed his path as a baller. Maybe it was Darius all along serving Silencer—I don't know, but I was soon to find out. I mean, it had to be him. Cornell was right in the middle of the hood where the bureau collected all the surveillance on him.

We set the party date for that Saturday night, inviting some people from Cornell and the weight customers we were serving. I wasn't sure if should invite Jackie or not because of the crowd, but I invited her anyway. I told her the party was going to be at Martt's and she could come if she wanted to.

Saturday came around fast, and we hadn't bought anything for the party. We didn't want to wear anything we already had, because that would be a disgrace, for we had money, and we had to always stay fresh with our gear. It was sign to others that we were balling. After we took care of a little business that morning, we decided to drive to the big mall in Johnson Creek. The Johnson Creek Plaza was huge. It had every store you could think of. There was Tommy Hilfiger outlet, a Guess outlet, a Nautica outlet, and a host of other discount shops. This plaza even had a mini-rollercoaster in it. It was so big it would take at least an hour to walk around the entire mall. We didn't want to spend much time, so we went directly to the stores we wanted to buy something from. The first store we went to was Gap, where we bought some fly button-up shirts. Then we went to the Kenneth Cole outlet to buy a few pairs of pants. The last shop we went to was the Shoe Depot, where we bought some shoes to go with our fly outfits. We left the mall with over $800 worth of merchandise each.

The drive to and from the plaza was two hours and thirty minutes, plus our shopping time. This left us pressed for time, so we had to hurry to get to the barber shop for a crisp cut and clean shave. After all that, we had only thirty minutes to make it to the club for our introduction from the guest DJ we'd hired to keep the night crunk. Silencer had surprised us with a limo, which picked us up from each location. We didn't even know about that, but it was tight. We had an all-black stretch Lincoln with pitch-black tinted windows. The inside had a mini-bar and TV. The night was going to be one to remember.

The line at the club was long, as usual, but we had VIP, so we didn't have to wait. We handed out VIP cards to selected people (Jackie being one of them). On the way in, we seen Tanisha, Shelly, and Erica in the line, so we took them in with us. I was hoping that Shelly didn't come so she wouldn't make a scene if she seen me with Jackie. I knew Jackie wouldn't trip because she was too much of a lady for that. Oh well, it was too late to worry about that. When we got inside, I told Shelly the truth. I told her I was involved with somebody that I loved and she was in the club with us. I asked her not to trip if she see me dancing and talking to Jackie, and please don't mention us. I had to use some reverse psychology on her by telling her she was the one who said in the beginning she didn't care if I had somebody. All she want to do is fuck. She responded, "Boo, don't worry. I'll be a lady. Just remember who do it better."

It was only ten o'clock, so the place wasn't packed yet, but it was getting there. There was mostly ladies in the house and a few men. The ladies got there early because it was free drinks for them as long they got there before eleven o'clock. Matty, who Silencer knew (unsurprisingly), escorted us back to our VIP section. He had the best VIP section I had ever been to. It was the size of a master bedroom and dining room put together, partitioned off with tinted bulletproof glass. We didn't want to make the girls stay out of the VIP, but if it weren't for Tanisha doing what she did for us, they would have been. The tables in the room were rectangular black stained glass with burgundy plush leather chairs. There was stripper pole in the middle of the room, surrounded by velvet soft couches—I guess just in case the ladies felt the need to let loose from the drinks and weed smoke that would be going on. The caterer had a bottle of champagne and Hypnotiq on every table. We bought the stuffies to put out. We had rolled twenty-five the night before to keep them fresh. We placed them in the refrigerator, wrapped in saran wrap. As time passed, the club started to get crowded. More and more people were filling the place. We could see out of the room, but the people couldn't see in. Gazing around the room, I seen almost everybody trying to see inside.

In the next instance, when I looked out, I seen Jackie walking back towards the door to get in. Feeling a little tense but calm, I went to greet her as the bouncer opened the door for her. I greeted her with a hug and a big wet kiss on the lips, tongue and all. We walked over to the table to take a seat and do the introductions. I went around the tables, which we had joined together.

"Jackie, this Shelly, Erica, and Tanisha. You already met Dirt, Red, and the infamous Silencer."

They all said their hellos. Silencer said, "You know you got a player on your hand, don't you?"

Jackie smiled and went along with the program. "I don't care, as long he as he know I'm number one and he treat me that way."

Silencer told me, "Man, you better keep her. She a good one."

The room became packed, but there was still enough room for everybody to have a good time, with two tables still empty. I didn't know who the tables were for, because I seen everybody that we normally associated with. I didn't want to be nosy and ask who the tables were for, because we were there to have a good time, not talk about business, but I was curious. A short time after my curiosity had moved on to the good time we were having, in came a group of ladies, with three well-suited men clinged on to their arms. The men each dapped Silencer's hand, then nodded at the rest of us at the table while the ladies just waved and jiggled to the bumping of Too Short. I was nervous as hell but kept my composure. Then I saw that one of the men was none other than who else Darius Brown.

If this wasn't some lucky shit, I don't know what is. I had been trying to pin them together for a year, which really should have only taken one month, and it finally happened. Darius took the center seat on one of the couches surrounding the pole, while his entourage, except for one, seated themselves in the other seats. The one that didn't was a nicely shaped caramel-complexioned lady. She started dancing close in front of Darius, taking off her top, exposing some firm breasts. She then started taking off her panties and putting them back on, teasing the onlookers. After another of Short's songs came on, she finally took them off, bending over to show her perfect round ass, which was hiding the string of her thong. The pole became her toy for the moment, as she climbed up and slid down with her legs spread open so everyone could see the lips of her vagina peeking out of the too-small front.

By now, the men in the room were having a hell of a good time smoking, drinking, some even sniffing what appeared to be a powdered substance up their nose, and watching a nice strip show by some beautiful women. Even the ladies in the room were watching the show. Tanisha was slightly turned on, as she rubbed her hands around the bulge in my pants and nibbled on my ear. Shelly and Erica was just commenting on the ladies' bodies, talking about how tight they was and how they wished they had them so they could be getting paid. Silencer told Shelly, Erica, and Tanisha that whichever one of them went up there and did something freakier than the last lady did, he would pay them five hundred dollars. Erica didn't buy it, but Shelly and Tanisha asked, "You for real?"

He said, "Hell, yeah."

They both then got up and walked up to the pole. They began kissing each other, then taking off each other's clothes. I was amazed at what I was seeing, as I remembered the conversation we had earlier in the old spot, Shelly saying she wasn't into that humping-coochies shit but look at her now. I know the effects from the weed and the drinks she consumed may have played a part in her going up there, along with the lure of five hundred dollars, but I really think it was to tease me.

They got fully naked as Too Short's song "Cocktails" played. Laid out in front of the couches in the sixty-nine position, they began eating each other out. Darius and his cohorts were having a real good time watching while doing some freaky shit of their own over there. I wasn't sure, but it looked like he may have been getting his penis sucked by the thong-wearing lady. Jackie whispered, "Are you having a good time baby?" as she seen me watching. I laughed and said "Yes, but it ain't nothing compared to what you and me do." She just smiled.

Tanisha and Shelly finished doing their thing, getting a standing ovation from everyone in the room. Hesitantly, I stood up too, making sure Jackie motioned to do so before I did. They came back to the table, hands out, ready to collect their promised loot. Silencer kept good on his promise, giving them each five hundred-dollar bills. The party went on, although it was close to closing time now, 1:45 a.m. to be exact. The DJ announced last call, so I went up to get a drink for Jackie. I got her the special drink I got her the first time I seen her, the shot of Tang, shot of Hypnotiq, and squirt of lime juice. I was already too gone, so I didn't get anything. As she finished her drink, she told me how horny she was and how she wanted to do something special for me. I asked her what she wanted to do and when she wanted to do it. She told me she wanted to see me fuck another woman tonight. I asked her if she was serious and who. She told me Tanisha. She said, "I want you to ask her to come to the hotel with us so you could fuck her while we eat each other." I asked if she was sure and it wasn't the alcohol or weed she had smoked for her to tell me. Since when have I known her not to be? I was happy, so I did what I was told. I asked Tanisha in her ear if she would come to the hotel with us. She was hesitant but looked at Jackie. Told me, "You better make me cum" and said, "Let's go." The night ended with a bang.

11

T H E next day, I met Silencer at the spot. We were both sluggish as hell from the hangover we suffered. He told me he had a hell of a night. He said him, Dirt, and Red took Erica and Shelly, along with three of the ladies that was in Darius's party, back to the spot and had some crazy sex going on. He told me they took turns fucking the girls. After telling me the details, he said to me, "I know you had a good night too. I know you took Tanisha back with you and ol' girl, huh."

I said, "Yeah, man, that shit was off the chain too." We made a few moves that day before heading over to see Dirt and Red.

Once over there, we found them sitting on the porch, smoking with Solo and his boys. They were more friendly now, showing us respect—I guess because Dirt had whipped one of their mans and they knew we was strapped up real tight. That's one thing money and power buy you in the streets, *respect*! I stayed on the porch partaking in the weed smoke while Red and Silencer went inside to discuss some business. I kept my eyes on Solo and his boys with my hand close to the 9 mm Glock that was under my shirt, just in case they broke bad on us, but everything remained cool.

After a while, Silencer came to the door and called all of us in. He told us all to take a seat after he took a seat on the arm of the lounge chair. With everybody seated, he began by telling Solo and the rest of the soldiers with him if their going hang with us, their going have to put in work. "He said, This some serious business we in, and ain't no room for weakness or pussies, so if anybody ain't ready to be down for life, leave now." They all stayed, so it was on from there on out.

He told Solo that since he was heading the show, he got to be the first one to prove himself by doing a job he had lined up. There was this dealer upstate who owed him some money. Solo was to go to the dude house, tie him up, torture him, and bring back the money and work he kept there in the bathroom closet. Solo took the job. To do the work, the car had to be stolen so it could not be traced back to any of us. Silencer had been putting in work for so long he was considered an OG, so he knew exactly how to do almost every crime you could think of. Solo decided to take Peanut with him. Peanut was his top man because he was real muscular and menacing looking. He was a born soldier—had the tattoos and the dumbness to go along with them, not to mention he was pitch black. I think if anybody seen him walking down the street by themselves at night, they would cross the street.

Later that night, they set out to do the mission while the rest of waited at the spot, chilling. They came back with the shit they set out to get, just like told. It was good having them now because they could do some of the dirty stuff Silencer wanted done, so I wouldn't have to. Not that I was scared, but I was already in too deep. I didn't want to have to hurt anybody physically. After counting up the money and strip-searching the two, Silencer bagged it all up to take with him home. I stayed for a little while longer, just hanging out with them, smoking on the blunts that was being passed around and drinking Tang. I left, going to Jackie's place, feeling real good. Before going, I just drove around, windows down, to get some warm air that was blowing and listening to the music playing. It was late, not many people on the street, so I just drove, thinking about what I got myself into, about Marcy and the kids, especially the hurt they must be going through, and what I'd become. I hadn't had time to reflect in months. This just felt real good. I hopped on the expressway and drove to the state line and back before getting to Jackie's house. Jackie was already asleep, so I didn't wake her. I just pulled off my clothes, then got into bed beside her.

The next morning, we met up at the weed spot. Silencer called me on my cell phone before I left, telling me we had some important business to take care of, which required taking a trip. I was hoping he didn't mean killing nobody, because I would never go against the oath of "protect and serve" I took as a police officer and bureau worker, not to mention God's word. I didn't care how deep under I was to go. I just couldn't do that unless my life was in danger.

I wasn't too anxious to find out what he was talking about, but I knew I would. I pulled up to the house at the same time as he did, so that was good. I didn't miss anything, just in case it was a trip to get rid of me because he found out I was an agent. When we got inside, I was relieved when he told us we were all going to Las Vegas on a road trip. He said we had to pick up some packages we needed to keep the business going. I knew now he worked for Darius, because I learned from wiretap recordings that is where Darius got his product from and that this was some heavy stuff we were going to pick up. Darius was connected to some Mexicans down there who controlled the flow of cocaine coming up through Milwaukee.

We were to leave out tonight. Silencer was taking Solo, Bones, and Dirt with him in the truck. I was to take Peanut and Red with me in the Buick. Before leaving, I went to the apartment to put some more information in the case file and pay Mrs. Holland the rent before I went to Jackie's to tell her I'd be back in a couple days. I called Mrs. Holland and told her the rent would be on the table. She could just come in to get it when she came over because I was in hurry and I wouldn't be there. I then went to Jackie's, which was really mine too. I just didn't want to think of it that way. I pulled up in the driveway, parked the car, and went inside. She was just coming out of the bathroom when I walked in the house, smiling pretty hard.

"You was just on my mind. I got something important to tell you."

I couldn't imagine what it was, so I asked. She calmly said, "Baby, we having a baby."

My heart dropped. I didn't want that. Nor did I know how to respond. I took a deep breath, put on a big smile, and said, "That's great." I told her I was glad and that was what we needed in our life to play it off, but really, I was thinking, *I'm in deep shit*. I told her I had to take a business trip to Vegas, leaving tonight, but I would stay if she needed me to take care of her. She told me to go, it's early on, so she is fine. She'll make a doctor's appointment when I get back. I asked her if she wanted me to bring her anything back. She said whatever I decided. I packed a few items and left to meet the fellas at the spot. We all gathered up and took our places in the vehicles, then headed off.

We arrived in Vegas thirty hours later. The trip went fast because we only stopped for gas. It normally would take a couple of days if you laid over and rested for sleep. I drove all the way to Colorado. Red drove the rest of the way. Vegas was hot as hell. It was hot in Milwaukee, but it was a desert, scorching heat beaming down on these niggas here. We arrived in the evening, almost at sunset, going to the motel close to the strip so we could get situated for the night. The next day, we were to meet the connect and be on our way. That night, we went to the strip to check out the casinos to do a little gambling and just chill. We all had money to gamble with, so we did a little gambling at different casinos to try our luck. None of us came out with anything.

We met the connect the next day, exchanged suitcases, and parted. The work got stored in the spare-tire compartment of the Buick so it wouldn't be easy to find in case we got pulled over by state troopers on the way back. During the drive back, all I could think of was this baby Jackie and I was going to have and what I'm going to do to support her. I couldn't leave Marcy, and I could not have both of them, because this was work, not real life. Somehow, I felt like I was stuck.

We pulled over in Illinois to get some gas to fill up for the last hundred or so miles, and I decided to call Marcy. I went to the bathroom to call her. At first, the phone just rang. Then I called again. When she answered, the first thing I said was, "Honey, I love you and I really miss you." I asked how were the kids and how was she maintaining. She told me everything was going fine, but she was worried because she got two disturbing phone calls the other day. I asked from who, and I was shocked when she told me. She said one of them was from this insurance salesman, Darius Brown, and the other from a timeshare woman named Jackie Tate. I became silent and hung up the phone.

12

W E made it back safely without anyone getting hurt. I was worried how I was going to pull the rest of this undercover stint off now that Marcy had been contacted by Darius and Jackie. My mind was racing all over the place. Did Darius know I was a federal agent? Did he just want me to know he knew how to touch me if I fucked up? Did he know where Marcy and the kids were living? Man, this some serious shit.

Now knowing Jackie was involved made things worse. I had to worry about her taking me out. I also had to worry now about the baby she was getting ready to have. Shit is complicated, but I am a veteran. I got this, even if it means I have to take someone out. I am going to ride this until the end. The only question now is: will it end?

The cocaine was taken to the stash house by Silencer and me while the rest of the crew went to spot. We made good timing. The city was dry, and we were the lifeline now. After a few minutes being in the stash house, Silencer proclaimed to me how much he appreciated my hard work and dedication to the family. He also told me he had someone for me to meet. I asked him who it was? He said the unthinkable: the man himself, Darius Brown. I asked who it was, as if I didn't already know. Silencer responded, "The man behind the whole operation, the numero-uno head honcho. Darius is who runs the city my man and we work for him."

I answered, "Cool, should I be nervous?"

Silencer responded, "No reason to be nervous. Just be yourself. Don't ask too many questions, and only speak when spoken to."

I didn't have a problem with that because I had to be cool anyway.

None of the kilos was opened until Darius arrived. It took about fifteen minutes for Darius to get there after us. He came in fresh to death, as he always was from photos of him from surveillance. He shook with Silencer and looked at me hard while walking to me.

"So this is the man Incognito I heard so many great things about, Silencer."

"Yes, that's him."

Darius approached me and said, "So you like working for me, man?"

I responded, "Yes, I didn't know I was working for you until now."

"Good, that means my crew is tight. Silencer put in a lot of work and years to be my second in command. He keeps shit tight for me so the weak and phony don't infiltrate us. You can be trusted I take it, right, Incognito?"

"Yes, sir," I replied.

Darius walked around me as if he was going to reveal what he thought he knew, but he did not mention anything about law enforcement, Marcy, or Jackie. He just stated if he had the choose between being busted and going to prison or death, he would choose death and would promise to come back from hell and destroy the police responsible for his demise.

He tested each of the fifty kilos by snorting a pinch from each to see if the purity was right. After liking and approving each, he would hit Silencer on the leg and say, "Good shit." Once he was finished, he said to me, "I will be on you, man. Don't fuck me over."

I replied, "I'm down for life, man. You can trust me."

He smiled and walked out. For some reason, I felt like I just crossed over, selling my soul to the devil and giving my life to the streets. I had to play it cool, however, so I could keep my life and save Marcy and the kids. For the rest of the hour, we were there. Silencer cooked the coke that was going to the projects and street-level dealers, and I packaged it for distribution while he set aside the kilos that were going to the other players in the game that was on our line.

I had to deliver the packages to the projects and street dealers, while Silencer delivered the product to the players. Dirt and Red was already in the projects, waiting for the new supply. I stopped there first to get an idea of how the new product was. We gave a sample to one of the customers who came to buy a dime. Dirt told the customer, "Try this shit, man. Buy one, get one free. You got to smoke it here." The customer loaded his pipe and took a long hit, then blew out the smoke. He didn't have to say nothing on how good it was, because we could tell from the sweat that beaded up on his forehead and how bucked his eyes got. The smoker shook his head, saying, "That's some good shit," then walked off. We all laughed at him before I hit the streets, delivering the rest of the packages.

The business was going smoothly out in the streets, so I was glad to have some time alone. I needed to strategize. I was still worried about Marcy. I had Jackie on my mind. I didn't know where I stood with the agency since I hadn't checked in for a couple weeks. When they told me I would have to go deep undercover I didn't know they meant this deep.

I thought, *I am sure I am violating some rules, so this case might not even make it through the legal system even if I get a bust out of it. Well, after my last drop, I will head to Jackie's place.*

I made my last drop on the other side of town to some youngsters on the come-up. They purchased three ounces of rock cocaine. It was a lot of money over on their side, but we had no rock houses there.

I was glad to finally finish, because I was exhausted. Being on the road for two days, on top of getting all the packages delivered, I wanted a hot shower, some hot sex, and a night's sleep.

It was a little after midnight by the time I arrived at Jackie's house. I didn't call her to let her know I was back or on my way, as

I wanted to catch her by surprise. I opened the door and walked in straight to the bedroom, where I seen her from the light of the television. I hopped in the bed on top of her, and she immediately went in for a kiss. After I told everything went fine, I asked her to take a shower with me. She agreed, and we got naked and went to the shower.

The water was very warm, just the way I liked it. Jackie washed my back, and I washed hers, looking at the nice backside she had, which was one of the things that drew me to her. She had one of the nicest asses I had ever seen. It wasn't too big, not to small, just right. It was just enough to place a cup on and jiggle when hitting it from the back, which is the notion I got while washing her. I began caressing her breasts as I washed her and grabbed her firmly in my arms. Now I had a full erection. I leaned her forward and slowly penetrated her vagina. She moaned a gentle moan as I entered, showing she was moist and had been waiting for me. The sex lasted about five minutes, and it was great. We both reached our climax and dried off before hopping in the bed, holding each other until we were asleep.

The next morning, I awoke to breakfast in bed. Jackie had made pancakes, bacon, and eggs for me, along with a glass of orange juice. While she was getting ready for work, I ate the breakfast and watched the news. I was shocked to hear there had been a homicide in the projects where we had shop. I was hoping Silencer or Darius was not behind it, but I expected they were. I headed out immediately.

I was in panic mode the whole way to the spot. I got there quickly, calming myself down before reaching the apartment. I rang the bell upstairs to enter, seeing Silencer, Do-Dirt, and Red. They had a blunt going around already. I accepted the half-sized blunt that was passed to me. Taking in two tokes, I told them I seen the news and asked who was that got who popped. Silencer told me a young cat they called "Ready-Rock." He was from the other side of the projects, but he tried serving customers on our side. The next question I asked was who did the job. Silencer responded, "A young pup on the come-up." I left it at that and finished toking on the rest of the blunt.

It has been a while since I checked in with the bureau, and I was really down under now that I had been sleeping with different women, smoking weed, and drinking, but it was all in the line of keeping my cover. I knew this was not protocol, but I really had to, especially now there was proof Darius ordered a murder and there was proof.

I will make the call to the bureau to arrange a meeting with my superiors so I can update them and plan an exit now that Marcy had gotten a call from Darius and Jackie—and since Jackie's miscarriage. I have nothing to keep me tied to this case.

Thursday at 8:00 a.m., I had to fly in to see Marcy and make the meeting. The flight is a straight shot four hours. I could be in and out without Silencer, Jackie, or Darius even knowing. I will tell Jackie I need to do some things at my place to keep things kosher. Darius and Silencer won't be up so early.

I called Marcy to have her and the kids pick me up from the airport. They were very excited to see me, as I was just excited to see them. I almost didn't realize I was married to her and had a normal life. I had to break character. I stayed with them for an hour or so before heading to the restaurant for the briefing.

When I got there, the looks on the faces of my deputy and captain spoke volumes. I knew they were upset. However, the reports, pictures, and tapes I threw onto the table eased the tension and anger. There may have been a little distrust also, for I was in too deep. My captain said, "I am pulling the case. You have to come out."

I replied, "I just need a month, and this thing can be big."

He asked if I could wrap it up sooner because it is getting too dangerous.

"You know they called your wife."

I replied, "I know, but I can't get out yet. I want to make sure they don't get to her by being on the streets. I am sure Marcy and the kids are safe. They don't know for sure. Just speculation."

He replied, "Okay, but get this done. Be there when the bust goes down so it can be natural. You need to be taken out of harm's way. The DEA is going to be in on the bust. They have the connect in Las Vegas, the project crew, and the sister. After all this is over, Marcy, the kids, and you will be put up in a house in the department's witness protection program. It's over, you hear me."

I replied, "Yes, thank God."

I caught a flight back to Milwaukee right after the meeting. It was 2:30 p.m. I went straight to the projects once the plane landed. I met up with Silencer and the crew to finish up the case. I had one last piece to put together, the murder suspect.

Later that night, I asked Silencer if we could talk about some business alone if it wasn't a problem. He said sure. Once we stepped off, I asked him about the young pup. I asked him if I could meet him because I had some work for him. His expression was skeptical.

"What, you working on the side outside the crew?"

I replied, "No, but I got a little problem around the way with a prankster."

He said, "Okay." He told me the young pup was Red. It was a test to see if he had heart enough to make general.

Blown away, all I could say was, "Word." I was now ready to end this.

Later that night, I called the captain and told him who the murder suspect was, as well as his new rank, but I still needed to get Silencer on a murder or two so he would turn against Darius. He was the one who knew the most and could do the most damage. Faced with double-life, I knew he would turn. After talking to the captain, all I could think about was the orders Darius gave before we left Vegas. Let me break them down so I can put them in the file.

"Silencer, when we get back home, I want you to take care of homeboy that was short on the count before we came on the trip all right."

"No sweat. I got you, boss. You know once I get the word it's over for any muthafucka that come against the crew."

"Yeah, I appreciate that too. Just be clean with it."

"Red, you get the product out like never before. This new shit gone put us on the map. We gone have the whole region coming to us for they re-up."

"Do-Dirt, I want you to gather some new members for the corners and trap houses. Scooby, you gone work at the new store we opening in the mall—a ladies' clothing line, upscale. Incognito, my main man, you and me about to get real close. You gone go across state to set up shop and be the one to open new markets in the tri-state area. Shit about to get real major for us fellas. Y'all good?"

"Fosho," we all answered in accordance to Darius's liking.

I was anticipating gaining more of Darius's trust. I was in, and now knowing Jackie was apart of the organization and was on to me on to me, I had to keep shit tight.

"Boss, I ain't gone let you down. I know we gone open up Kenosha, and Racine, Minnesota, and Indiana, but I was thinking about expanding to New York, Philly, and Boston—even Detroit."

Darius replied, "You right. That's exactly it, bro. You got this. Then we can move more kilos and become a black cartel ourself. From here on out, our crew gone be known as 'Trump Tight Family.' Let's get it."

That was playing in my mind, over and over. I was now really in, and I had Silencer tied to the upcoming murder.

We didn't waste no time getting down to business. I was on my way to Minnesota with five kilos, driving by myself across interstate lines, so I was extra careful not to get pulled over on the interstate. I made the four-and-forty-five-minute drive in six and a half hours to be extra careful. I got there and called Darius to let him know I made it and the location of the stash spot I got. It was an apartment on the north side of town, real low key and out of sight so nobody could be hip to it. I would have to find one person to give a sample of work so they could put word on the street that it is some new product on the street that was not cut and guaranteed to bring back your money when you whip it.

After getting situated in the spot, I had to get some furniture and clothes, so I went on a shopping spree. I had to keep it simple, kind of like the apartment I rented from Miss Holland. This time no agency stuff, just some real smooth shit to fit the part of a regular dude. I got a nice sectional, and nice bedroom set with a big-ass ill TV, and a laptop for the living room and bedroom. Also, got a few things for the fridge and bathroom. Now that the apartment was fixed, delivery was set up for the next day, so I was ready for the club. I drove around town looking for the nightlife. I went downtown to see what was up. I didn't want to be at the so-called ballers places. I needed to be at the real ballers spots.

It was this popping spot I found called Red Corvette. There was a line outside around the corner, so I figured it might be a good place to start. From the line, it looked like a mixed crowd, and they were playing hip-hop. I parked a block away and walked to the joint. I walked to the front of the line, like I usually do when I go to the club to see if I could get in by paying the bouncer. I talked to one bouncer, told him I had a hundred dollars if he let me walk in. He accepted and took the money. I was in, just like that. If you want to play the part, you got to spread money around like it ain't shit. If I want it, I get it. I am really deep cover, in character. Once inside, I worked the room, peeping out the baddest bitches in the club to the players. One thing working undercover and the training from the bureau taught me: you can always tell a real player from a nobody by the body language and character. You see, being a player is kind of like being an agent: you can never let them see you sweat. You must keep your cool at all costs. You want to get rich and have fun as a player, but as an agent, you want to get your subject.

There were some players in here now. I just had to get in contact with one, but I don't want to rush it, so I had to get a girl to use to connect me. I'll find one to buy a few drinks to take to the hotel after the club close so we can fuck, and she can point me in the right direction.

Bam, I see my target.

I peeped a nice redbone across the way. She eyed me, so I know she interested. She just got a body like she done smashed a few of these cats in here and she know just the ones that got that bread and ain't afraid to spend it. I walked to the bar and ordered a drink.

I stayed there and looked out at her to make sure she knew I was watching and was interested. As I was drinking my drink, we caught eyes again. I put my drink in the air and pointed to it to say let me buy you a drink. She knew, because after the song playing went off, she left her girls and walked up to where I was standing. I introduced myself as Incognito and asked her name.

She said, "I'm Success. Nice to meet you, Incognito."

I said, "Likewise. What you drinking?"

"Whatever you buying."

"Cool." I told the bartender to make a special drink. I said, "Give me a double shot of Tanqueray with a shot of Hypnotiq and a splash of lime juice." As the bartender was making the drink, Success and I began talking, more just small talk, like you come here often and shit like that. I said I was here from Chicago so this my first time here. She said I know cause I'm here all the time and I never seen you in here before. I said so you remember faces. She said something like that.

Her drink came, and as she tasted, she said, "This is good. What do you call it?"

"I call it pussy wetter."

She laughed and said, "I see what you on. I like that."

We began talking more, and she asked how long I was gone be in town. I said for a week. She said cool. She asked what I do for a living and I told her I was an investment banker. I asked her what she did. She said I work for a bank too. "I do customer service." I was like, coincidence, huh? She finished her drink and asked if I wanted to dance. I said sure. I finished my drink and went to the dance floor. She was a better dancer than Jackie and even looked better than Jackie. She just wasn't as homely as Jackie. We danced for three songs straight before heading back to the bar. At the bar now, it was a little crowded, so we had to wait to order our drinks. Finally at the front of the line, I asked if she wanted the same thing, and she said yes. I got the same drink for the both of us. While sipping our drinks, she said, "You know, the bar about to close, and I don't have a man, and you here for a week. I don't see no ring, so what's up?"

I said, "What you mean?"

She said, "You know I'm feeling you, and this drink got the right name, because my pussy real wet. I was thinking we can go to the hotel and get nasty."

"If you sure, I'm with it."

"Good. Let me go tell my girls I'm going with you, just in case you might be a killer or something, Mr. Investment Banker. Be right back."

I was in just that quick. I was gone fuck her good and ask her if she knew any ballers, cause on the side I move weight. I needed to get the five kilos off in a week and be out. As we were walking out, I asked if she was riding with me. She said of course. I had my whip, and it was nice so I knew she was gone be impressed. It was a black-on-black Mercedes S500 with the AMG rims and black tint, something to make her pussy wet even more. As we were walking to the car, she said, "You better make me cum."

I said, "You don't have to worry about that. That's what I do."

Got to the car, she said, "This all right. Typical for men in your line of work."

The night ended with us being at this nice hotel she took me to, not far from the club we were at. I fucked the shit out of her and got some real nice head. She made me come twice and even swallowed.

The next morning, we woke up at the same time and did the same thing, checked our phones, and headed for the shower. While in the shower, I asked her if she knew any ballers in town and wanted to make two thousand dollars for introducing me to one or two of them. She said, "I can do that." She asked me what I was selling. I told her some A1 cocaine from the West Coast. She said, "Cool. Give me your number. I will call you later."

I said, "Cool, but remember, I am only in town for a week, so they got to have the bread. I am willing to give a sample though, to show I'm legit."

"No problem, baby. I got you."

We got out the shower, got dressed, and I dropped her off at her house. It was a nice apartment building not too far from the hotel downtown.

I called Darius when she got out the car, and I drove off to tell him we were in. I made a connection. He was like, "That's what's up, bro. You moving, my nigga."

I said, "You know I'm doing my part, but I'll hit you again when I'm out the product and on my way back with the money."

He said, "Cool, and by the way, I got something to tell you, but not now. It can wait until you get back."

I said, "Bet."

I went to the apartment to wait for the furniture and for the call from Success. I was at the apartment, and while waiting for the furniture, my phone rang. It was the agency, calling on a blocked, untraceable line. Somehow, Captain knew where I was and told me the local bureau knew of me and okayed my jurisdiction into the city. He also told reminded me to get this done. I said, "I know, Captain, and thanks." I briefed him on the club and Success and what was going to take place in Minnesota. He just reminded me to get it done and that I would be introduced to an agent working in Milwaukee before I left. I said okay and hung up to answer the door for the furniture delivery.

It was about thirty minutes for them to get everything in and set up, and they was out. I was now waiting on Success to call. She was right on time. She called like an hour after the furniture people left. I answered in anticipation of her call. She said, "Hey, baby."

I said, "So I'm your baby?"

"Yep. Just that quick. That's how I move when I like somebody, but it ain't often that happen, and plus, nobody ever put it on me like you did last night."

I said, "Okay, I enjoyed it too."

"But about that business. I got a buyer that says if its A1, like you say, he need five kilos. He want to meet in a hour at my spot."

I said, "Word. You ain't setting me up, are you? And do you know him?"

"Yeah, he really cool—legit. I been knowing him for a minute now, and besides, if I was setting you up, you think I would do it at my crib?"

I said, "You got a point. I'll be there in an hour. What's the apartment number?"

She said, "Thirteen o two. See you soon."

I said, "Bet."

I got to her place in forty-five minutes to look around outside the block and in front before it went down to make sure no cats were out lurking. I didn't want to have to shoot anybody and make a mess of this case here. She buzzed me up as I got inside she kissed me and said he called me to say he is about five minutes away.

"Just relax."

She had some mellow music playing, something different but cool. Five minutes later, the doorbell rang. It was the dude I was to serve. He came up and entered the place and shook my hand as she introduced us.

"Incognito, this Al. Al, this Incognito."

So I got right to it. I said, "My man, these five keys from the West Coast, no cut. I'm letting them go for $30,000 apiece. If you come back for re-up, we can negotiate a lower price then."

He didn't hesitate. He said, I got $200,000 on me, so that's cool. Success got the money machine to count it right over there. Let's do this."

She said, "I will bring it over here so y'all can make sure the count is good and exchange real quick so I can go to work."

While she was getting dressed for work, I ran the money through the counter—all hundreds and fifties and twenties: $150,000. I gave Al my number and said, "Be in touch." He told Success later and left, I stayed behind and gave her $2,000, as agreed.

She threw it on the table and said, "Let's fuck before I go." We fucked and came together. She said, "So, when am I going to see you again?"

I said, "Tonight when you get off."

"For real."

"Fo sho. I want to spend as much time with you as possible before I leave town.

She said, "Okay, I feel the same way."

We parted ways. Later that night, I met her back at her house around 11:00 p.m. I was waiting downstairs for her when she pulled up. She pulled alongside me and said, "Let me park in the structure. You can come down too. I have two spots."

I followed her into the garage. We headed up to her condominium apartment, which was really nice for a customer-service representative. I was really tired, so I took my shoes off and sat on her couch. She said, "Make yourself at home. I have to go get more comfortable."

I said okay. As she walked towards the back, she yelled, "Oh yeah, remember I told you I had something to tell you. I will when I come back."

She came back in some sweat pants and a T-shirt with a badge around her neck. So I wouldn't blow my cover, I asked, "What the fuck is this? You a cop?"

She said, "No, I am a federal agent, and I know all about you. Why you think I went with you from the club? All of them girls I was with were agents too. Al is one of the main players here we been on for over a year. I needed a good connect to get on him. I am glad for you that you came."

I was in shock. She said, "Didn't your captain tell you you would meet a local agent before you left? Well, here I am. I know you been under for a long time. So have I. It gets hard sometimes, but we are serving a good cause, and we can never blow our cover. This case will be over soon—now for me, and from what I hear, you too. Al moves five kilos every two weeks, so you need to get back to Chicago to re-up for when he calls you. Let's go to sleep now, and we'll debrief with my superiors here tomorrow."

The night ended with us going to sleep, holding each other in her beautiful California king bed.

Bright and early in the morning, around 5:00 a.m., there was coffee made and breakfast. Success, or Agent Peterson, was in the kitchen, wearing appropriate field close, listening to CNN and FOX News simultaneously while her comrades were drilling me. I was told since we already had their subject linked to narcotics trafficking, he would go down, but to get him even more buried in shit, we needed to get him on conspiracy charges, so I needed to sell him another load by the end of the week. I said cool, Success could hook it up since it was her case.

"I'm leaving after this to go take my subject his money and re-up on product. I'll be back in twelve hours, thirteen tops. Be ready."

Agent Peterson yelled, "I stay ready. I'm the original don dodda from the island of Kingston, Jamiaca, rude boy. Be safe out there, baby." That shit turned me. I never heard it like that before, but I was out.

When I turned onto the ramp to enter the freeway, which was three blocks away, I got a nice speed up and called Darius. He answered, "What it do? Please tell me you already out of that new-new."

I replied, "And you know it. I'm on my way back right now to count and re-up. Dude want five more bricks. He be moving five every two weeks of that normal, but he ain't never had nothing like this. Why it is going so quick? The killer part is this broad I fucked arranged the whole meeting and took care of the count with me for $2,000. She a bad little broad work in banking."

He said, "Long as the money good and the product is wanted, I'm cool, but watch her."

"Yeah, I'm already knowing. But on the real, I'm gone need some of that Harold's ten wings salt and pepper with mild sauce on the side. See you soon, roadie."

13

ON my ride back, I turned the ringer off my phone, put on the Eightball & MJG Coming Out Hard CD, sparked one up, and rode. This how I stayed in character, relaxed, and strategized. I drove to Chicago to get some wings from Harold's a chicken joint off 87th before driving back to Milwaukee I also wanted to know what Darius wanted to tell me. But for now, these salt-and-pepper wings gone be fire, as they always do. Drop that mild sauce on them boys and drink my cold pop. Heaven, my nigga. They knew me at this joint, cause I'm always here spending big, usually because I get orders for everybody. My food was already made, still hot and ready to go. I paid the cashier a tip and was out the door. Ate five wings before I drove out the parking lot. The other five riding to the spot. On full now—time to conduct business.

Silencer and Darius was already there chilling. Just finished eating the same thing I had plus an original hoagie. If you ain't from the Chi, you probably never had a hoagie, but you missing. Darius went right in with the news he had to tell me before we even picked up the money bag.

"Hey, homeboy, you remember Red?"

"Yeah, of course."

"Well, he ain't with us no more."

126

I asked, "Did he get popped? Is he going to snitch? He ran off? What's up?"

"The nigga buried in the buoy in Louisanna with them gators. Homeboy was shorting the count, so Silencer had to silence him."

I said, "Better him than me. Let's count this money so we don't have them problems."

Darius smiled. "My nigga, my nigga."

We counted $150,000 cash, the same way, all hundreds and fifties and twenties. All there. Darius then asked if they had a Bank of America there in Milwaukee. I said no but something like US Bank, where ol' girl I had help meeting the new buyer works.

"She like a personal banker customer-service rep that can give us inside information if we open an account and deposit large amounts."

"Yeah, that's what we need. Work that out."

"I'm on it. Just give me the $150,000 to start when I leave tonight with the other five kilos. Boss, you got my word on God I'm with you till the end."

"You better mean that shit, nigga, cause that's what it is—til the end. 'Trump Tight Family.'"

"Cool, after this run, I want to make my way to Detroit do an in-and-out type thing, though. Same with Saint Louis. Cool? We gone need 100 kilos next time. Well, I'm out. Hit my line if something changes or you need me."

Back on my way up to Minnesota to finish this piece up with the 5 kilos and $150,000 in the trunk in a duffle bag under some shopping bags full of clothes to hopefully make one last trip here for the undercover part of the case. I drove to the apartment spot to check in on it. Everything was cool. I then called Success to see if I could meet her at work to get the keys to her condo. She didn't answer, so I left a message.

"Hey, baby. Is your boy. I was wondering if I could crash at your place tonight to just chill and get ready for this next move. One more night, and I can be out of your hairs, you know. Peace. Hit me back."

"I waited for about ten minutes, then the phone chirped. It was her."

"Hey, silly. Just heard your message. Of course you can stay over. Meet me at my job in five minutes. I am walking out now. It's slow, so I took an early out. The address is 5639 North Browndeer Road. I'm waiting."

"On my way, pretty lady. Bye."

I got there as soon as I could, seven minutes, to see her waiting talking to some other cat in a Chevy Camaro. She got in her car, and I followed her. It took us about thirty minutes to get to her condominium. We got there and parked. While waiting for the elevator, I asked who was that cat at her job.

"One of Al's boys. He going down too for dealing, moving a nine-piece or so."

"Okay, so you got something to eat upstairs?"

She said, "Yeah, me. It's sweet and juicy tonight too."

"Well, that can be second. What about some soup and broccoli?"

"Yeah, I think I might. That don't sound bad. You gone make us some?"

"Sure thing."

We both washed ourselves in her deluxe multi-head shower, with water coming from everywhere, hitting every crevice of your body. Felt good. We washed each other up and just kissed and touched, no sex, then got out to go cook and eat. I made some potato and kale soup with some broccoli on the side. After eating, we talked. I wanted to get to know her a bit. I asked her if she was married. She said yes.

"Does your husband know what you do?"

"Yes."

"He don't mind?"

"No, he is a special agent too. He works financial crimes."

"Wow, okay, that's cool. You have any kids?"

"Nope. No time for that. Besides, I can't have any ever since the abortion."

"Oh."

"What about you? Married?"

"Yes, with two kids."

"She like what you do?"

"She appreciates it, but she worries all the time and gets scared. That's why this might be the last case I work."

She replied, "I see. Might be mine too. Then where do we go?"

"The bureau's protection program, I guess. It might not be so bad. We could probably train new agents."

"I never thought of it that way. Well, I'm sleepy? You want to crash? Sure."

We made passionate love before going to sleep. You could tell we both needed real affection from someone we trusted and loved, since we haven't been with our spouses in months and years. I kissed her on the forehead goodnight and rolled over to go to sleep.

Tomorrow would be another day to meet Al so I could serve him the second time to make the case. This time, he would have to be on a wire, so the bureau in Milwaukee gave me a recorder to use once the deal went down. He was to meet me at 5:00 p.m. Once the code word was signaled, the agents would come into the apartment to bust us. Al was on time, and everything was set up as planned. The code that I was to use was "You all good?"

After the deal went down and the money count was there, I said the code, and sure enough, the agents stormed the apartment. They took Al into custody right away by slapping him into handcuffs and telling him what time he was faced with and asked if he wanted to work for us right away. Al took the deal and offered to work for us to keep his freedom. He was well advised. If he spoke anything of what went down, he would be arrested and would definitely serve ten to twenty years in federal prison.

14

NOW that we had the Milwaukee area working, I took back to Chicago to let Darius know things were going just fine and I tapped into the new market. It was on to the next market, which was Detroit and Minnesota. The only problem was we only had twenty kilos left, so I would have to take ten so I could tap into the two new markets, in and out. This time, I wouldn't set up an apartment, just stay at the hotel.

I got to Darius and gave him the money and the progress. But instead of doing the typical, I had informed the bureau of what was going down, so they arranged for me to have two undercover agents already working the area to arrange a buy. It was set up that Al our new contact in Minnesota told them about the product and me so they wanted to meet me and buy five kilos each. I got the call while Darius was counting the money and told him he should come with me to see how I operate. I was trying to impress him and get this case closed by putting him in another state for major trafficking. I wanted him to be known as a narcotics enterprise so he could get mandatory life in federal prison.

He agreed to come and would have to set up another meet with the cartel in Las Vegas, this time to do a deal for 100 kilos. Things were going sweet. Progress was being made, and I was never happier. I just hated that Jackie was going to go down too, but hey, she was involved, so it was my duty to get charges on her too. I just had to figure out a way to get her to cooperate by giving her a lesser money-laundering charge. Speaking of Jackie, when Darius and I got back, I would have to spend some time with her and act like nothing happened between me and Success, play it like I handled the business alone.

The next day, we headed to Detroit and Darius gave Silencer the in-charge key so he could handle things until we get back. It was not that long of a drive, so we should be in and out, just make the deal and be on our way. I was still being cool not to let Darius know I knew about the call to Marcy, because I didn't want to blow my cover. The heat was on, and I was sure he was just speculating out of paranoia, but I wasn't taking any chances.

We made it to Detroit in no time. Met the buyers—or agents—at their location and did introductions and exchanged product for money. Darius was in charge the whole time, just the way we wanted it. He even told them that he could get them whatever they needed. This was too nice. In and out and back on our way to Chicago.

We got back later that evening. I went to Jackie, and Darius went to his house. He took the money with him to gather the count for the re-up with the cartel. Now I knew that he kept all the money at his house, so we knew where to hit first and second.

The next few days things went smooth and quick. Do-Dirt had gathered four young soldiers to run the trap houses and the corners with the other soldiers, and Scooby had got the store running nicely. It was now time to head to Vegas. This time, the whole crew wouldn't go, just me, Darius, and Silencer. We drove two cars. Me and Silencer was in one, and Darius drove alone in the other. This was perfect. I made sure I played all the murder music Silencer liked to listen to so conversation would be minimal. This was going to be a thirty-two hour drive there, and coming back would take a little longer because we would need to drive a little slower.

While driving, we got a call from Darius to tell us plans had changed. He got a call from the connect that there was a drop in Houston and we could pick up there. That was another trafficking charge in another state. The fire was about to be lit under this nigga. It was time to end this already before somebody else got killed and before Darius decided to get out or got even more suspicious. We made it to Houston and met the connect at a mechanic garage they had set up as a front. The money was counted. The product was exchanged, and there was a bunch of talking of how the next time they would bring it to us. We parted ways and made our way back to Milwaukee.

Driving only to stop for gas was our task as the product was in the car with us, and Darius was out in front as a decoy car. We stopped about six times but finally made it back to Milwaukee. It was late, so we took the product to the stash spot, smoked a blunt, and had some drink, talking about how this breakdown was about to go down. I had everything I need to inform superiors. I left to go back to my apartment to put the finishing pieces on the case. I saw Miss Holland had been by the apartment because there was a note on the door. I was about to leave all this behind. I immediately called my captain and told him to be at the stash house at 9:15 a.m., when Darius would be inside, breaking down everything. They then would have Silencer there as well. The other agents would have to pick up Do-Dirt, Scooby, and Jackie. It would have to be a simultaneous roundup.

I was ready. I didn't even sleep all night. The next morning was here. I went to the stash house as planned and noticed agents in the vicinity, waiting. I got there around 9:05 a.m. Silencer was already there. We were just waiting on Darius. Darius was a little late. I was worried he got an inside tip that it was going down, but he showed up at 9:35 a.m. He sat down and rolled up a blunt, and the agents came rushing in. He was startled, in disbelief. The 100 kilos were on the table, right in front of him. The agents served him with his warrant and pictures of him with the other agents and me. He and Silencer were in cuffs. This time, there was no deal for Darius, and the only thing Silencer could do was say he was the second-hand man and Darius was in charge.

They both were taken to headquarters without incident. Darius's house was raided, where $1,000,000 in cash was impounded, along with guns and jewelry. The corners were rounded up. Scooby was taken into custody, and Jackie was picked up on her way to her car, leaving for her office.

In the end Silencer was given seventy-five years for the three murders, Do-Dirt was given fifteen years for possession with intent to distribute and being apart of a crime organization, Scooby was given ten years for the same charges because he had no previous record, and Jackie was given five years plus ten years' probation. For the big finale, Darius Brown was given life in federal prison for running a major drug organization and drug trafficking across state lines. This was a long case, but I could now say, "Case closed."

I returned home to Marcy and the kids and got a medal for my hard work and dedication. I started training new agents who came into the bureau and lived a modest life thereafter. I never went back into the field again.

About the Author

ROBERT Johnson is the author of both fiction and non-fiction works. He began writing in 2006, and his first book was a memoir. He enjoys telling stories he feels can intrigue and inspire others.

Printed in the United States
By Bookmasters